HIGH SPIRITS

HIGH SPIRITS

Neil Jordan

faber and faber

LONDON · BOSTON

First published in 1989
by Faber and Faber Limited
3 Queen Square London WC1N 3AU

Photoset by Parker Typesetting Service Leicester
Printed in Great Britain by
Richard Clay Ltd Bungay Suffolk
All rights reserved

Extract from 'Chantilly Lace' by J. P. Richardson on page 70
reproduced by permission of Peer Southern Organization.

British Library Cataloguing in Publication Data
is available.

ISBN 0-571-15454-9

Neil Jordan

Two years ago I read an article about an Irish tour operator who was propagating the idea of haunted holidays in Ireland for American tourists. He would meet them at Shannon Airport in a black limousine, dressed appropriately in top hat and cloak, and lead them round a series of ruins where unemployed members of the Irish theatrical profession would pose as ghosts. This intrepid gentleman seemed to encapsulate all the virtues of his race and mine: enterprise, ingenuity and an inexplicable attachment to an utterly useless idea. It was the last attribute that was particularly attractive to me. The thought that an idea or enterprise should have any practical application other than it's own internal logic – dare I say, its beauty – has been and should be anathema to all of us.

I subsequently met the general manager of the Irish Tourist Board – a cousin of mine, equally scornful of the tyranny of fact – who told me that this particular enterprise received more international press than any other during his tenure but that, in keeping with the beauty of the idea, nobody came. What struck me was the metaphoric possibilities of this business, how it encapsulated in a nutshell two of our great national characteristics. First, the unsurpassed ability to conjure up alternatives to that awful condition – The Way Things Are. And second, the absolute indifference to their practical application. The end result being that purest of institutions – the useless one.

Once one frees an institution or an enterprise from the tyranny of usefulness or fact, one does come up with all sorts of intriguing results. For instance, a thirty-two-county republic whose writ runs in only twenty six. Or, a national language spoken by nobody. Or, a state legislature wherein divorce is only available through ecclesiastical authorities who are themselves opposed to it. Or, a government which actively propagates the emigration of its working class.

I could go on, but won't. Suffice it to say, that given that the end in view was to be another great monument to uselessness, a motion picture, the end of that end had to be in some way uplifting. The useless idea had to, probably through its own inherent uselessness, triumph. And so I proposed the following scenario:

Hero has inherited an ungovernable fact – an ancient, rambling stately hotel in the West of Ireland.

Is presented with an intractable problem. The ever-present rain, the rotting floorboards, the dripping rafters, the mildewed beds repel even the hardiest tourist. No one wants to come.

(Now observe with what devilish cunning the canvas has been sketched – the setting: quaint, intriguing, Irish . . . The dilemma: heartbreaking, in a word . . . The palpable feel of bated breaths, the one inescapable question – what will he do???)

Hero imagines a perfectly useless solution. Pretend the place is haunted, advertise it as such, thereby making virtues of its shortcomings. The dry rot, the rising damp, the cobwebs and the mildew all become absolute necessities to the ectoplasmic ambience of the place. Get the staff to provide the ghosts . . .

(And here is where the minor themes come in – those quaint, enchanting vignettes, so deftly illustrating the charm of the Irish character, wherein the staff surpass themselves in useless inventiveness: that Brunellian tangle of wires which make Katie the servant girl fly like a banshee; the awesome simplicity of the rig whereby the four-poster bed turns and rises of its own accord; the clinical ingenuity with which Eamon the handyman bounces his image through a series of mirrors into successive rooms. And thus far please note the gamut of emotions traversed – from Perennial Despair (the beginning) to Inspiration (the idea) to Frenetic Activity and Hope That Will Come To Naught (the inventions) all leading to the next turn of the narrative vice – Chaos, the Pathos Of Failure (inevitable, but who would have thought it?).)

Hero sees beautifully crafted, immaculate ingenuities collapse around him. Guests (for now there are some) almost decapitated by flying banshees, crushed by falling beds, insist on leaving. Hero, being Irish, drowns his sorrows in drink. Then at his darkest hour, unbeknownst to him, comes Triumph. The guests find they can't leave. Ghosts, real ones, all related to him, emerge from the woodwork. Playful ghosts, horrific ghosts, romantic ghosts. Hero observes his dream come true, in spite of his best efforts; sees his guests become embroiled in a comedy of horrors, a truely necrophiliac romance with the ancestral dead.

(And so from that blackest of emotions, Despair, comes, in succession – Absurdity, Fear, and that great current cinematic staple, A Sense of Wonder. And in the end, the triumph of the Useless.)

The problem with comedy, however, is that people not only demand that it is funny, but ask the awkward question – is it really funny? Or its variant, is it funny enough? The corollary of this question is never asked, strangely enough, of other genres. I have never asked of a tragedy, is it tragic enough, or of a thriller, is it thrilling enough. Only comedy, it seems, is so inescapably tied to its banal condition. And so, when I brought the idea round that web of financiers, producers, executives in charge of development us martyrs call the world, the question cropped up continually. With a most sinister variant, which was generally whispered behind my back when about to visit that great American institution, the bathroom – even if it is funny, can he direct comedy? It proved useless to point out to them that the tragic and the comic modes could well be two sides of the same coin, that awfulness becomes most awful when it is almost comic. Even to point out to them the comic possibilities of my first film, *Angel*, in which a deaf mute goes to a dancehall to listen to a saxophone player and is shot by a club-footed assassin who is later discovered working in a shop that specializes in orthopaedic shoes.

On a more serious note, I am convinced that every film nowadays must have two purposes. The ostensible purpose, the one spoken about at that other great American institution, 'the meeting', that comes to the forefront in publicity campaigns, that probably, in the end, brings people into the cinema. Called by various unspeakable names – the elements, the concept – it is a dialogue that one must partake in, a game, almost, but never quite, a lie. And the secret purpose, the one you can never mention if you want the film made, but which constitutes the real reason for making it. In the case of *High Spirits*, it was my need to make a film in Ireland, drawing on a particular strain in Irish literature of the absurd and fantastic. Ireland is a country with almost no cinematic tradition, but with a grotesquely rich literary one. Movies cost money, but words and fantasies are free. I thought of the metaphysical ironies of James Stephens; of Flann O'Brien, in all his various personae – most particularly in the persona of Myles Nag-Copleen and his catalogue of useless inventions; of that strand in Irish theatre with its roots in melodrama and its branches in supernatural farce – a kind of marriage between the slapstick of music-hall comedy and the rich fantasy of the peasant tradition. One finds it in the later O'Casey; in George Fitzmaurice, a little-known Kerry playwright who mingled figures from local legend with characters from silent movies in his farces; in Dion Boucicault, despite his worst excesses. I thought of Bram Stoker, whose derelict house I used to pass on my way to school, at the Crescent, in Marino. But perhaps the most austere, the most complete ghost behind this script was that of a contemporary of Stoker's, Oscar Wilde. A film which becomes in the end a necrophilic romance, in which a living couple fall madly and blissfully in love with a couple who have been dead for centuries can only aspire to his sublime sense of fantasy and cynicism.

I mention all of this not to make any great claims for the script that is to follow, which will read awkwardly at best, given the amount of characters it has to deal with, the speed with which they ring the changes and the amount of special effects needed for those changes to happen, but to give some insight into its sources.

As to the story of the making of the film which sat uneasily and at times subversively on the script that gave rise to it, it entailed the usual catalogue of frustrations, delays, encounters with the sublime and the ridiculous. Suffice it to say that it was made with as great a group of artists and technicians as I could ever hope to work with. And that for a time it placed me in the unique position of being the only European director in Los Angeles who had not got a project at British Columbia. Hence the following poem . . .

LINES WRITTEN IN DEJECTION

The baby-faced executive
has only so much time to give

the vps file in through the door
your current script lies on the floor

a tasteful parquet, newly done
to signify the Brits have come

they ask why it's not like your last
you tell them that emotion's past

they say your forte seems to be
film noir and not filmed comedy

I thought I'd try my hand at farce
you mumble, thinking what these ass-

holes need to hear is repartee
so try a line or two to see

how it goes down and when it dies
you hit them with some other ploys

it's visual so all the laughs
come out of what you'll photograph

the bed that falls down through the floor
that's not been seen on screen before

the bus that rises from the bog
means more than all the dialogue

a deft amalgam of what's best
The Quiet Man, Ghost Goes West

the classic form, the current theme
the surreal logic of a dream

then seeing their attention wane
you try another tack again

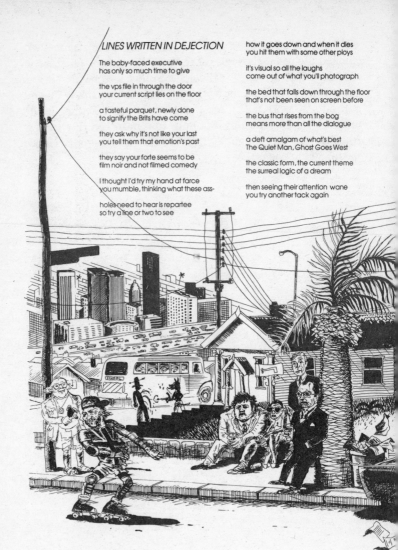

ILLUSTRATION BY JOHN HEWITT

the gore, the blood, the sex, the crack
the fun is necrophiliac

they smile politely, not too much
promise that they'll be in touch

we'd love to work with you someday
if not on this we'll find a way

I like your suit, what's your hotel?
you hear the elevator bell

you swing your budget rent a car
left on Santa Monica

you crash a light, then hit a kerb
and scream the solitary verb

the bimbo on the left hand lane
screams it back at you again

your driving's bad, your script's a mess
your credit-card is creditless

you're melting slowly in the haze
that typifies Los Angeles

you threaten to, if things get worse
go back to writing awful verse

you only ever said you'd come
so postcards might impress your mum

so buy one while the going's good
your loving son in Hollywood

NEIL JORDAN

High Spirits opened at The Odeon West End cinema, London,
on 9th December 1988
The cast was as follows:

MARY	Daryl Hannah
PETER PLUNKETT	Peter O'Toole
JACK	Steve Guttenberg
SHARON	Beverley D'Angelo
MIRANDA	Jennifer Tilly
MARTIN	Liam Neeson
BROTHER TONY	Peter Gallagher
PLUNKETT SENIOR	Ray McAnally
MALCOLM	Martin Ferrero
MARGE	Connie Booth
EAMON	Donal McCann
MRS PLUNKETT	Liz Smith
KATIE	Mary Coughlan
BROGAN	Kenneth Mars
Casting	Susie Figgis
Special Visual Effects	Derek Meddings
Music	George Fenton
Editor	Michael Bradsell
Production Designer	Anton Furst
Director of Photography	Alex Thomson
Executive Producers	Mark Damon
	Eduard Sarlui
	Moshe Diamant
Co-Producers	Nik Powell
	Selwyn Roberts
Screenplay	Neil Jordan
Producers	Stephen Woolley
	David Saunders
Director	Neil Jordan

INT. CASTLE CORRIDORS, DINING ROOM, PUB AND
CORRIDOR. NIGHT
*Camera tracks down a long, dismal corridor, past tatty kitchens, a
lounge, mouldering dining rooms, etc. Various members of the hotel
staff are seen.* CHRISTY RING, *the* maître d', *in an evening suit he
seems to have slept in for the last fifty years;* SAMPSON O'TOOLE, *a
massive, muscular chef with red hair and long sideburns, a
Walkman draped round his neck; young* DAVEY, *the world's
unhappiest bartender . . . past stone corridors, wine cellars that
were once dungeons. We come to a door through which we hear a
voice, abject and humble.*

INT. PLUNKETT'S OFFICE. NIGHT
PLUNKETT *drinks from a bottle of Jameson's as he talks. All
around him are pots and pans, catching the dripping rain coming
through the ceiling.*
PLUNKETT: Mr Brogan? Mr Brogan? Mother, would you get
    off the line, I'm calling Jem Brogan in America, yes, in
    America, Mother – so please get off the telephone. Ah, Mr
    Brogan – this is Peter Plunkett calling from Ireland. Now
    I know you must be worried about last month's payment,
    but there's been a postal strike – yes, the same one as last
    month – but I can assure you that if it lasts much longer I

I

will take this cheque which I am holding in my hand and personally ferry it across to England – shut up, Mother! If I say there's been a postal strike – that's my mother, Mr Brogan, she gets confused at times – Mother – for the last time, get off the line – Mr Brogan – please – I don't think that kind of language is necessary –

(*As he listens, he takes a rope and strings it over a crossbeam.*)

So, what you're saying is if I don't come up with the money in three weeks you'll foreclose and take over Castle Plunkett. Have you heard of the quality of mercy, Mr Brogan? No? I see. Goodbye, Mr Brogan.

(PLUNKETT *puts down the phone, takes a rope from his cabinet, stands on a stack of chairs and places it round his neck. As he's about to jump, his mother comes down the stairs.*)

MOTHER: Oh, that's it, take the easy way out.

PLUNKETT: Mother, this is not the easy way out . . .

MOTHER: Just 'cause you haven't a guest in the place, the family home's about to be taken over by that guttersnipe Brogan . . . Your father's tearing his hair out with worry . . .

PLUNKETT: Father's been dead for a decade, Mother.

MOTHER: What about your grandmother? How do you think she feels?

PLUNKETT: Mother, she's dead too.

MOTHER: So! She's still upset . . .

PLUNKETT: Well, I apologize profoundly to the ghosts of my ancestors for the mess I've made of their home . . . (*Idea.*) Mother, just how many ghosts are there here?

MOTHER: Well, apart from your father and granny Joyce, great-aunt Nan and Uncle Tobie, Jeremiah who died in the plane crash, and that sweet Elizabethan lady, not to mention . . .

(PLUNKETT *leaps down and embraces her.*)

PLUNKETT: Mother, what an idea – what a tourist attraction. Ghosts . . . ghost tours . . . (*Bellows*) Katie – take this down . . .

INT. CASTLE MAIN HALLWAY. NIGHT

A decrepit castle corridor. PLUNKETT *strides through it dictating, pulling the noose off his neck.*

PLUNKETT: Haughlin Castle, a superbly restored edifice in the heart of the incomparably beautiful Irish countryside, also known to be the most haunted place in the Emerald Isle.
(*His staff gather round to listen.*)
Here the dead outnumber the living . . .

INT. CASTLE UPPER CORRIDOR. NIGHT

PLUNKETT *turns a corner, into an even more decrepit corridor.*

PLUNKETT: Each room lovingly preserved in an impeccable state of decay . . . Not a cobweb touched, not a skeleton turned . . . Meet the ghosts of your ancestors, the spirits of yesteryear, on All-Hallows. We can promise you Banshees, Pookhas, wraiths of all descriptions.

INT. A FOUR-POSTER BEDROOM. NIGHT

PLUNKETT: The one thing we won't promise is a good night's sleep.
(*He leaps on the bed, which collapses on top of him. The base falls out. He pulls* KATIE *into the wreckage with him.*)
KATIE: But, there are no ghosts.
PLUNKETT: I know. That's where you come in.

EXT. DCIO. DAY

A British Caledonian DC10 flies over the Atlantic.

INT. PUB. DAY

PLUNKETT *is on the phone, nursing a bottle of his beloved Jameson's.*

PLUNKETT: Yes, Mr Wilson. We unconditionally guarantee the authenticity of every Haughlin apparition. We maintain the ectoplasmic ambience by preserving the environment of the castle – dry rot, cobwebs, selective damp. Ghosts need such things to exist.
(*A suit of armour slides towards him on roller skates.* JULIA *is inside it.*)
JULIA: Can't Katie do this and I do the flying virgin?

3

(PLUNKETT *slams the visor over her face, shutting her up. He
puts down the phone and goes towards where a makeshift stage
is being rigged to move of its own accord.*)
PLUNKETT: Shaping up well, boys.

INT. FIRST-CLASS CABIN. DAY
SHARON *is asleep with her eyeblinds on.* JACK *is uncorking a bottle
of champagne.* SHARON *speaks without removing her eyeblinds.*
SHARON: Jack, what is this?
JACK: To us, honey. To Ireland. Your homeland. Maybe we'll
get to see the Loch Ness Monster.
SHARON: That's Scotland, Jack.
JACK: Who cares? Cheers.
(*He uncorks the bottle and it froths all over her.* SHARON
whips off the eyeblinds.)
SHARON: Christ, Jack. I've taken two Valium and now you
want to drown me in champagne.
JACK: You don't want it?
SHARON: No. (*She pulls her eyeblinds back on.*) Next thing

4

you'll want to have sex.
(JACK *turns with the glass to the lady behind him – an ancient woman, with her earphones on.*)
JACK: For you, ma'am?
(*She smiles sweetly, shaking her head.*)
I suppose sex is out of the question?
(*She smiles sweetly again, shaking her head, not hearing.* SHARON *doesn't answer.*)

EXT. CASTLE. DAY
An old school bus is being painted black and grey with stylized cobwebs by the hotel staff. On the ground beside the bus is a shop mannequin which is being made to look like a gruesome corpse by SAMPSON *and* DAVEY.
DAVEY: Why is he holding potatoes?
SAMPSON: To show he's the ghost of somebody who died during the famine.
DAVEY: If he was starving, why didn't he eat the potatoes?
(SAMPSON *thinks about this for a moment.*)
SAMPSON: We'll put some spots on him and say he died of the pox.
DAVEY: Or maybe we should cut off his head.
(*A large sheet of glass slices down from the garage roof, neatly decapitating the corpse. The locals look upwards at:* EAMON McCARTHY *on the roof of an outhouse. He's arranging large sheets of glass to face the castle.*)
EAMON: Anyone dead down there?
DAVEY: Only the corpse, Eamon.
SAMPSON: What are you doing up there?
EAMON: Genius, boy. Wait till they see it.
(*Camera pans up to a window where* MRS PLUNKETT, *Plunkett's mother, is watching.*)

INT. MRS PLUNKETT'S ROOM. DAY
PLUNKETT *walks jauntily down, whistling, into his mother's room.*
PLUNKETT: Mother.
MRS PLUNKETT: It won't work, Peter.

5

PLUNKETT: What won't work?

MRS PLUNKETT: This ghost business. Your father's dead set against it.

PLUNKETT: Father's dead, Mother.

MRS PLUNKETT: Doesn't make him deaf and dumb into the bargain. He's seen what's going on here and he's very disappointed in you.

PLUNKETT: Can't you leave Father out of this?

MRS PLUNKETT: Your father turns in his grave every night. To think of the hopes he had for you and the castle. And you with not a guest in the place.

PLUNKETT: Mother, there is a planeload of Americans arriving. And it's this ghost business that's bringing them here. I'd be grateful if you'd stay in your room during the course of their visit.

MRS PLUNKETT: Don't you want me to scare them? Booo!!!

PLUNKETT: No, Mother. You stay here with Father.

(He leaves, throwing his eyes to heaven. As he does, a slight breeze opens MRS PLUNKETT'*s wardrobe door. An old suit dangles conspicuously from a hanger, swaying slightly.* MRS PLUNKETT *lifts a sherry bottle from table beside her and pours two drinks.)*

MRS PLUNKETT: Have a drink, dear.

INT. DC10 TOURIST-CLASS CABIN. DAY

MALCOLM CLAY, a parapsychologist, is sitting next to his wife, MARGE. MALCOLM *is taking notes on Plunkett's brochure.*

MALCOLM: This Plunkett fellow lists eighteen separate phenomena and suggests there are a great many more. I did all the research and found no mention of Haughlin in any of the literature. If just one of these apparitions has even the remotest particle of reality to it, I'll eat my doctoral thesis. Page by page.

MARGE: Oh, it doesn't really matter, does it dear? The point is, we're on a family vacation.

MALCOLM: It matters to me, Marge. Exposing frauds in the field of the paranormal is my profession.

(He hears giggling in the seat behind him and turns to his children. WENDY, *thirteen,* WOODY, *ten, and* GRAHAM,

6

eight. WENDY *is pretending to vomit in the vomit bag, cracking the boys up.*)
Stop that, Wendy! I thought I told you to read the Fodor book on Ireland.

WENDY: We don't want to do that.

MALCOLM: Well, you'd better do it, because I'm going to give you a pop quiz when we get there.
(*The children groan.*)

WENDY: (*Under her breath*) What a dorkus.

MALCOLM: What did you say, young lady?

WENDY: Nothing.

MALCOLM: Then read.
(MALCOLM *turns away.*)

WENDY: 'The Irish are a gregarious people. They cannot stand to be left alone. They must always be talking to their friends . . . unfortunately, they all have really bad potato breath and pick their noses and wipe their boogers on their pants.'
(*The kids all crack up.*)

INT. ANOTHER PART OF THE PLANE. DAY

MIRANDA KUHL, *a drop-dead, twenty-year-old beauty, is sitting next to a guy who thinks he's really suave.*

SUAVE GUY: So what do you say you and me have a little 'lay-over' in Dublin, foxy lady?
(*He puts his hand on her thigh.*)

MIRANDA: Don't tell me. Let me guess. You're married, you've got three kids, you hate your job and you haven't made love to your wife in three years because you're probably impotent. Hey, pal. Take a major hike!
(*She slaps away his hand, gets up and walks down the aisle, looking for an empty seat. She finds one next to* BROTHER TONY, *a devastatingly handsome young seminarian.*)
Excuse me, father. Is this seat taken?
(BROTHER TONY *looks up at her, stunned. He shakes his head in silence.*)
(*Sitting*) Thanks, father. I was sitting next to this jerk who's been hitting on me since New York.

BROTHER TONY: It's 'brother', actually. Brother Anthony. I'm

7

not a priest yet.

MIRANDA: Well, I've got this problem, brother. I've got this
body jerks like that can't take their eyes off. (*She leans
towards him, voluptuous and mock innocent.*) But now that
I've found myself a priest, I think my problem's solved.
(BROTHER TONY *tries to keep his eyes off the 'problem'.*)

BROTHER TONY: Ah – how is it . . . solved?

MIRANDA: Priests aren't like that, right?
(BROTHER TONY *nods emphatically, shakes his head, then
nods again.*)

BROTHER TONY: Yes. I mean no. I mean I'm not a . . .

MIRANDA: So I'm going to this castle where there's a ghost in
every toilet . . .
(*She notices the brochure in* BROTHER TONY's *lap. She
smiles deliciously.* BROTHER TONY *squirms.*)

EXT. CASTLE. DAY
Belching clouds of exhaust, the bus roars off down the driveway,
EAMON *at the wheel. The bus bears the legend:*

HAUGHLIN CASTLE
WHERE THE DEAD COME ALIVE
HAUGHLIN VILLAGE
POP (LIVING) 123
POP (DEAD) 722

*The bus passes a very unsteady figure on a white horse. We realize it
is* PATRICIA, *in a body-stocking, wearing a lurid red wig. As she
approaches a tree, a hand grabs down and pulls the wig off her
head. It is* KATIE, *dressed like a banshee.*

KATIE: I think I should play the tart on the horse, and you
should play the hag in the tree.

PATRICIA: I think I should go home.
(PATRICIA *guides the horse towards* SAMPSON, *her father. He
is arranging a series of stuffed animals along the castle gates.*)

SAMPSON: Did you remember to bring your old man a smoke?

INT. DC10 FIRST-CLASS CABIN. DAY
STEWARDESS: We have begun our descent into Connaught
Regional Airport. We will touch down in approximately

8

fifteen minutes.
(*Another stewardess walks down the aisle, collecting customs declaration forms.*)

JACK: (*Looking at Sharon's form*) Sharon, aren't we on a holiday?

SHARON: Yes. Why?

JACK: Under purposes of visit, you put down 'business'.

SHARON: (*Beat*) Slip of the pen.

EXT. CONNAUGHT AIRPORT. DAY
A tiny airport in the West of Ireland. The DC10 roars down and lands with a noticeable bump. It is the only plane in sight. The rain everywhere is torrential.

INT. DC10. DAY
JACK *and* SHARON *walk towards the exit. Outside is a torrent of rain.*

SHARON: Damn it. Do we have to walk? Can't we get a car or something?

EXT. CONNAUGHT AIRPORT. DAY
They deplane into the rain. JACK *is ecstatic, the rain pouring down his face.*

JACK: No wonder this country is so green.

EXT. TERMINAL. DAY
The Americans emerge and look with amazement at: EAMON, JESSIE *at his side, howling like a wolf, by the bus.*

EXT. COUNTRYSIDE. DAY
The Haughlin bus drives through the Irish countryside.

INT. BUS. DAY
EAMON'S *driving leaves a lot to be desired, swinging wildly around the narrow corners, blithely unconcerned about his passenger's safety. He announces the glories of the passing countryside over the bus microphone in a sepulchral voice.*

EAMON: On our right, we have the Haughlin bog. Home to more grisly murders than any spot on the globe. The

9

fierce O'Flahertys would pile down from the
Cnocmealdowns raping and pillaging women, children,
nuns, priests.
(*He winks to* JESSIE.)

EXT. APPROACH TO CASTLE. DAY
*The bus approaches the castle. Lightning crackles overhead and
thunder rolls.* KATIE, *in her banshee costume, is perched among the
branches of the blackthorn tree above the road, drenched and
miserable. She sees the bus approaching.*
KATIE: Sampson! Sampson! Here they come!
(*We see* PATRICIA *a long distance off, in a copse of trees,
clinging nervously to the horse.*)

INT. BUS. DAY
EAMON *is warming to his role.*
EAMON: And the blackthorn tree from which the Brogan
        banshee is rumoured to howl . . .
        (JACK *looks at* SHARON.)
JACK: Brogan? I wonder if you're related?
SHARON: (*Sneezing*) Who cares?

EXT. BLACKTHORN TREE. DAY
In the tree, KATIE *sets up a dismal wailing and begins waving her
arms. She loses her balance and falls. She hits the bus roof with a
massive* THUMP!!

INT. BUS. DAY
*All the Americans stare upwards, genuinely alarmed. They can
hear her terrified screams.* EAMON *warms to the sound, ignoring the
source.*
EAMON: And the banshee's howl draws out the restless spirit of
        Lady Amelia Purefroy galloping naked on her white
        mare . . .

EXT. APPROACH TO CASTLE. DAY
From the castle grounds comes PATRICIA *on the white carthorse,
which is rearing, now totally out of control. She clings to it in terror,
in a damp white body-stocking with her lurid wig in a hopeless*

tangle. The horse charges directly towards the bus. On the roof, KATIE *clings desperately spread-eagled over the sunroof.*

INT. BUS. DAY
SHARON *screams, looks upwards and sees* KATIE's *squashed visage, as she claws for a hold on the sunroof.*
JACK: (*Shouting*) Look out . . .
   (*The Americans turn and see the carthorse charging straight towards them, with* PATRICIA *holding on for dear life.* EAMON *waves to* PATRICIA, *then turns the bus, casually, at the last moment. The bus skids to the left, then to the right, out of control.*)

EXT. CASTLE. DAY
PLUNKETT, *at the portico entrance, sees: the bus spinning towards him,* KATIE *clinging desperately to the sunroof. He ducks, as the bus crashes through the portico, dragging the canvas with it.* KATIE *goes flying in the air, and lands on top of* PLUNKETT. *The bus slews on its way, past the castle, down an incline, crashes through the undergrowth, out of sight.*

INT. BUS. DAY
The Americans scream in terror, as the bus crashes through the undergrowth. The kids wide-eye each other.
WENDY: Awesome.
WOODY: Really.

INT. LAKE DAY
A placid lake front, with a jetty, below the castle. The bus crashes through the trees, bumps down the jetty, breaking all the struts, and stops at the last possible moment. A beat. Then the jetty breaks beneath it, and the bus sinks into the lake.

EXT./INT. CASTLE. DAY
PLUNKETT, *covered in mud, tries to console* KATIE. *From the trees comes a group of very wet, slime-covered Americans, carrying their sodden luggage.* SHARON *looks particularly miserable.*
SHARON: Jesus Christ. This is the end of the world.
PLUNKETT: (*Sotto voce to* KATIE) Best foot forward, Katie. (*He*

11

grins manfully and steps forward.) Welcome to Castle
Haughlin.
(*He makes a sweeping, theatrical bow. The Americans glare
at him balefully.*)
Please make yourselves at home.

EXT. CASTLE. TWILIGHT
*The castle broods in the twilight, against the lurid sky. The rain has
stopped and the winds whip across the bog.* SAMPSON *leans over
the swimming pool with a large net. It ripples with thousands of
fish. He takes an armful of the fish – whiting – from the pool and
strides towards the castle to cook dinner.*
INT. MRS PLUNKETT'S ROOM. NIGHT
PLUNKETT *is serving* MRS PLUNKETT *tea. A wind whips through
the casement window, throwing it open. The wardrobe door bangs
repeatedly.* PLUNKETT *goes to shut the window.*
MRS PLUNKETT: It's a warning.
PLUNKETT: What's a warning?

MRS PLUNKETT: About the American who's come to stay . . .
PLUNKETT: They're all Americans, Mother.
MRS PLUNKETT: One of them brings no good.
(PLUNKETT *bangs the wardrobe shut. Then, from somewhere off, a loud shrieking is heard.*)
What did I tell you?

INT. JACK'S AND SHARON'S ROOM. NIGHT
JACK *is lying on a rickety four-poster bed, surrounded by other pieces of warped furniture, covered with a fine film of grime.*
SHARON *screams from the bathroom.* JACK *leaps off the bed and runs towards her. Through the shower curtain,* JACK *can see Sharon writhing as if she were fighting someone off. Cold water pours from the shower head.*
JACK: What is it? Did you see a ghost?
SHARON: (*Screaming*) There's no hot water.
(JACK *hands her in a towel.*)
JACK: Well, at least it's authentic.
SHARON: Authentic what?
JACK: I mean ghosts don't use much hot water, do they?
(SHARON *throws herself on the bed.*)
SHARON: What a dump.
JACK: (*Lying down beside her*) C'mon. Let's make love and give the ghosts a show.
SHARON: Jack, is that all you ever think about?
JACK: Don't do it for me, Sharon. Do it for your ghostly ancestors.
SHARON: They would have had clean sheets.
(JACK *sits up, rebuffed.*)
JACK: Look, Sharon, I wanted to go to St Bart's. You were the one who wanted to come here because it's where your people are from. OK, we're here. Now I agree it's far from perfect. And if I was with anyone else but you, I'd probably slit my wrists. But if I wasn't with you I'd probably slit my wrists anyway. We're together, and that's what counts. Let's give it a chance. And if you still can't stand it after a couple of days, we'll catch the first plane out of here.
(SHARON *looks at him calculatingly.*)

13

SHARON: OK.
> (*He looks around the room, in the fading twilight.*)
JACK: But to tell you the truth, I kind of like it.

INT. DINING ROOM. NIGHT
Close-up of a portrait of a beautiful, innocent, wistful twenty-one-year-old girl with the legend MARY PLUNKETT, 1750–1771. *The shot opens up to reveal a large, splendid room, very old, beautifully authentic, spoiled only by a lurid yellow carpet. The Americans sit around the tables, waiting for dinner and expecting the worst.*
PLUNKETT *is at Marge's and Malcolm's table, pouring wine.*
KATIE *pours wine.*
MALCOLM: Mr Plunkett, what is whiting *en anglaise*?
PLUNKETT: That would be a lovely whiting with breadcrumbs.
MARGE: And whiting *en nature*?
PLUNKETT: Boiled whiting.
WENDY: What about the whiting *vapeur* stuff?
PLUNKETT: That, my dear young one, would be whiting . . . steamed.
MALCOLM: (*About to take a sip of wine*) And what's this? Whiting Bordeaux?
PLUNKETT: Very witty, Mr Clay. Very witty.
WOODY: Mom, so where are these ghosts?
GRAHAM: Bo–r–ring! I want to see one now.
MALCOLM: Boys, I'm afraid there are no ghosts here.
PLUNKETT: Ah, a cynic, Mr Clay.
MALCOLM: No, a parapsychologist from Harvard University, Mr Plunkett.
> (PLUNKETT's *stunned reaction*. SAMPSON *serving* BROTHER TONY *and* MIRANDA *their soup du jour*.)
SAMPSON: Whiting *bisque*, Madame?
MIRANDA: So, I was seeing this guy and he's a devil worshipper, right? Well, he's a hairdresser really, but he devil worships on the side and we booked this dumb tour 'cause, you know, he likes ghosts, corpses, dead gerbils, that kind of thing, and he ran off with this Buddhist monk. I mean how was I to know he was gay? So what about you, are you a gay too?

14

BROTHER TONY: No, I'm, uh, not.

MIRANDA: Just kidding. Trick question. So what are you doing here?

BROTHER TONY: Well, I thought I'd take a vacation in the Isle of Saints before I made my final vows. A sort of spiritual retreat.

MIRANDA: Yeah, well I've taken a vow myself. I've sworn off guys. For a while at least . . . But you're not a priest yet.

BROTHER TONY: Not yet.

MIRANDA: (*Toasting*) Well, here's to keeping your vows.

(JACK *is quietly eating his soup, staring at the portrait of Mary Plunkett directly in front of him. He can't take his eyes off her.*)

JACK: Who's that?

PLUNKETT: Mary Plunkett. My great, great, great, great, great, great cousin. She died right here in Haughlin Castle, two hundred years ago.

SHARON: She couldn't take the whiting either?

PLUNKETT: Levity is out of place, Mrs Crawford. She was murdered. On her wedding night. By the hand of her newly wedded husband.

(SHARON *gloomily contemplates a menu composed entirely of whiting.*)

SHARON: What's whiting *meunière*?

PLUNKETT: I'm sorry, the *meunière* is off tonight. Might I suggest the whiting *en papillotte*?

EXT. CASTLE. NIGHT
The castle, spectral under a full moon. Tiny flashes like fireflies in the foreground. From one of the basement rooms comes the sound of singing.

INT. PUB. NIGHT
The Americans are gathered with a scattering of villagers, observing the local cabaret. KATIE *sings in her green costume, while* EAMON *plays the accordian. The locals sing happily and drunkenly. The Americans sing along, each as to their personality.* JACK, *most enthusiastic, and* SHARON, *stonily silent.*

KATIE: What foll the doll

Will you dance with your partner
Belt the floor your trotter shake
Wasn't it the truth I told you
Lots of fun at Finnegan's Wake
(*The song ends to limp applause.* PLUNKETT *comes on the stage with the air of a bad stage magician. Behind him,* EAMON, *in full view of the Americans, pulls some light switches. The lights change dramatically. A local child begins to cry.*)

PLUNKETT: The full moon has risen above Haughlin Bog. Those with nervous dispositions would do well to protect themselves. Bolt your doors. Lock your windows. Say your prayers. For tonight, they might be walking abroad – the cluricanes, the phookas, the banshees and the madrallams. Good night, sleep well . . . If you can . . . If you dare.
(*The spotlight goes out on* PLUNKETT *and the room is plunged into darkness. A moment later, the lights come up and the Americans find themselves alone.*)

MIRANDA: Where did they all go?

SHARON: Don't ask. They might come back.

MARGE: If there are any ghosts in this castle, I hope to God they put on a better show than this one.

JACK: Pretty scary, huh, kids?

WENDY: Did you see *Nightmare on Elm Street*? Give me a break!

INT. MARGE'S AND MALCOLM'S ROOM. NIGHT
In a bedroom of faded opulence, MARGE *is doing her nightly ablutions by a mirror.* MALCOLM *is preparing his paranormal equipment at a table by the window. Between them is a suit of armour.*

MALCOLM: I think this is going to turn out to be the most pitiful scam I've ever had the pleasure of exposing.

MARGE: Where's that nightie you bought me in the duty free?
(*There is a nightdress draped across a chair. The suit of armour picks it up and hands it to her. She takes it without looking around.*)
Thank you, bug bear. And look after these, will you?

(*She takes off bracelets, jewellery, etc. The suit of armour obediently takes them. As she undresses, she hands each article of clothing to the suit of armour, thinking* MALCOLM *is taking them.*)
I mean, you can put up with just so much, can't you? I don't think even ghosts, if there are any, could put up with this dump.
(*A massive commotion from her children can be heard next door.*)
Why can't they ever just go to bed?
(*She rushes to the door and goes outside. The suit of armour follows her.*)

INT. MIRANDA'S ROOM. NIGHT
MIRANDA *lies on her four-poster bed. She is watching TV, wearing a kimono over her shapely body. She lies back and stares up at the ornate top of the four-poster. The bed begins slowly to move on its axis. She doesn't notice at first, staring upwards. She sits up to look at the TV, but finds herself facing the window. She turns around, puzzled, faces the TV again, and finds it is changing position.*
MIRANDA: Jesus Christ. Major jetlag.
(*The bed begins to move faster. She clings to the arms, growing increasingly more frightened.*)

INT. BROTHER TONY'S ROOM. NIGHT
BROTHER TONY *sits at the window, reading his breviary. Such is his concentration that he doesn't notice the figure of* KATIE, *flying past the window in her harness, waving her arms like a demented cherub.*

EXT. CASTLE ROOF. NIGHT
SAMPSON *catches* KATIE *on her upward swing.*
SAMPSON Try knocking at the window this time.
KATIE: Do I have to?
(*He ignores her protest and flings her into the darkness.*)

INT. CLAY KIDS' BEDROOM. NIGHT
The Clay children are running around wildly, draped in sheets, pretending to be ghosts. MARGE *throws the door open. The suit of*

armour can be seen outside, covered in her underwear.

MARGE: You've got three seconds to get back into bed or you're all grounded!

(*The kids see the suit of armour behind her. It scares them half to death. They all dive for the bed and pretend instant sleep.* MARGE *goes triumphantly back out, thinking she finally has them under control.*)

EXT. CORRIDOR OUTSIDE MALCOLM'S AND MARGE'S ROOM. NIGHT

MARGE *strides back into her own room. Again, the suit of armour follows her. She opens her own door and slams it shut in the suit of armour's face. The suit grunts with pain.*

INT. BROTHER TONY'S ROOM. NIGHT

A loud scream sounds from next door. BROTHER TONY *looks in its direction, and so again misses* KATIE, *flying past once more, desperately trying to reach the window. The scream gets louder.* BROTHER TONY *recognizes* MIRANDA'S *voice.*

BROTHER TONY: Oh Lord!

(*He runs for the door.*)

INT. MIRANDA'S ROOM. NIGHT

BROTHER TONY *bursts in. In the background* KATIE *flies past Miranda's window, but he still doesn't notice. All he sees is* MIRANDA, *on the bed, whirling violently, clinging like a beautiful damsel in distress to the bedposts.*

MIRANDA: Tony, help me! Help me!

(*She reaches out an arm for* TONY. *He grabs it and falls on to the bed with her.*)

Can't you do something?

BROTHER TONY: What?

MIRANDA: Exorcize the mother!

(*She clings to him. She looks very beautiful and very desirable. He raises his eyes to heaven.*)

BROTHER TONY: Pater mei qui es in coeli –

(MIRANDA *buries her head in his shoulder.*)

INT. MALCOLM'S AND MARGE'S ROOM. NIGHT
MARGE *is standing by the bed.* MALCOLM *is still fiddling with his equipment.*
MARGE: (*Seductively*) Come to me, bug bear. Make me a
woman.
(MALCOLM *turns. As he does, a* WRAITH-LIKE FIGURE,
*looking suspiciously like Eamon, emerges from the wall,
passes through both of them, and disappears into the other
wall.*)
MALCOLM: Jesus H. Christ, was that phoney?
(MALCOLM's *eyes search around the room to see where it has
gone.*)
MARGE: Look!
(*She points to the window, where* KATIE *flies by once more.
Delighted to be seen at last,* KATIE *grins like a trapeze artist
and waves her arms. A scream of very real fear comes from the
kids' room next door.* MALCOLM *and* MARGE *rush for the
door.*)

INT. MIRANDA'S ROOM. NIGHT
The bed moves even faster. MIRANDA *is beginning to enjoy* TONY's
closeness. A groaning starts up below them. She clings tighter.
MIRANDA: Must be the ghost of an orgasm.
BROTHER TONY: There's no such thing.
MIRANDA: Hold me!
BROTHER TONY: I am!
MIRANDA: Tighter!
(*The groaning gets louder. She clings even tighter.*)

EXT. CORRIDOR OUTSIDE MALCOLM'S AND MARGE'S ROOM.
NIGHT
MALCOLM *and* MARGE *rush out of their own room, in terror.*
GRAHAM: Mom, we saw a ghost!
(*They see the suit of armour and stop dead. The suit, still
draped in Marge's underwear, begins to walk towards them,
menacingly.*)
MALCOLM: Oh, very nice. A pervert ghost.
WENDY: Mom, he's stealing your underwear!
(WENDY *grabs a vase and flings it at the suit of armour. It*

smashes. The headless suit continues to move towards them.
The kids retreat in terror. MARGE *screams.*)

MARGE: Do something, Malcolm! Do something!

INT. JACK'S AND SHARON'S ROOM. NIGHT

SHARON *is lying in bed with her sleep mask on.* JACK *is standing*
watching her, shirtless, in his jeans. He drops to his knee, like a
Casanova, with his arms outstretched. Of course SHARON *doesn't*
notice.

JACK: Hi. It's me, Jack. I'm your husband, remember?
　　(*Silence.*)
　　Maybe if I changed my name . . . (*He does the gesture*
　　again.) Hi. It's me, Simon. I'm –
　　(*From the wall, the same wraith-like* GHOST OF EAMON
　　emerges, heading straight for SHARON *as if to ravish her.*)
　　SHARON!
　　(JACK *rolls violently over on top of her to protect her. He*
　　lunges for the 'ghost' – his hands flail through it – and the
　　GHOSTLY EAMON, *making a gesture of abject apology,*
　　vanishes through the other wall. SHARON *jerks up in the bed,*
　　furious. She whips off her sleep mask.)

SHARON: Jack, how many times do I have to say no?! I'm
　　exhausted. We are not making love tonight!
　　(JACK *points in desperation at the wall.*)

JACK: But there was a ghost attacking you!

SHARON: That's the most pathetic excuse for having sex I ever
　　heard.

INT. CORRIDOR OUTSIDE MALCOLM'S AND MARGE'S ROOM.
NIGHT

The headless suit of armour advances towards MALCOLM.

MALCOLM *grabs an ornamental sword from a window ledge.*

MALCOLM: Lead on, Macduff!
　　(KATIE *flies by the window, grinning.*)
　　You bunch of frauds!
　　(*He heads for the suit of armour, sword at the ready. The*
　　headless suit retreats before him. As it does so, the GHOSTLY
　　EAMON *emerges from the wall, grins proudly and begins an*
　　Irish jig between them. MARGE *cowers behind* MALCOLM.)

MARGE: I think it's real.

MALCOLM: I'll show you real!

(*He flings the sword through the window. There is a loud crash of glass, screams from outside and the* 'GHOST' OF EAMON *vanishes.*)

Just as I figured. All done with mirrors. It's so obvious.

(*Curses, voices heard out of shot.*)

EAMON: (*Out of shot*) Nearly fucking killed me!

SAMPSON: (*Out of shot*) Goddamn Americans!

EXT. CASTLE. NIGHT

SAMPSON, *staring down at the wreckage of* EAMON's *ingenious mirror-rig, forgets to catch* KATIE, *flying up towards him on her harness. She wails, then falls down, now out of control.*

INT. CORRIDOR/GALLERY/SPIRAL STAIRCASE. NIGHT
The headless suit of armour is now running for its life away from the
Clay children, towards the stairs.
GRAHAM *and* WOODY: Kick his butt, Wendy!
    (WENDY *blind-sides the suit, sending it tumbling down the*
    stairs. GRAHAM *and* WOODY *high-five* WENDY.)
GRAHAM: Radical!

EXT. CASTLE. NIGHT
KATIE *flies through the air, swinging in terror.*

INT. MIRANDA'S ROOM. NIGHT
We see a series of winches attached to the four-poster bed above the
canopy going up through the ceiling. The ceiling is cracking
dangerously. A moment later, the ceiling gives way and DAVEY, *the*
barman, crashes down and falls through the top of the canopy,
landing between TONY *and* MIRANDA. *For one moment, the bed is*
still, and TONY *and* MIRANDA *gaze at* DAVEY *stuporously. Then*
the entire broken bed crashes down through the floor.

INT. JACK'S AND SHARON'S ROOM. NIGHT
They're in the midst of a furious row.
SHARON: I don't care what goddamn ghost it was! If I say I'm
    too tired, then I'm too tired. Now I'll need two more Valium!
JACK: Maybe if we made love more often, you wouldn't need
    your stupid Valium. Jesus Christ, Sharon, this was
    supposed to be our second honeymoon!
    (*And crashing through the window comes the hapless* KATIE
    who pummels into SHARON, *throwing both of them on the bed,*
    which collapses on top of them.)
SHARON: JACK!!!!

INT. CORRIDOR OUTSIDE JACK'S AND SHARON'S ROOM.
NIGHT
MARGE *and* MALCOLM *are nearly thrown to the ground by* SHARON
crashing out of her room, furious and imperious, followed by JACK
and the tearful KATIE. *Their babble of anger is silenced by*
tremendous crashing sounds coming from the stairway. They all rush
in that direction.

INT. TOP OF MAIN STAIRWAY. NIGHT
The Clay kids and the headless suit of armour all tumble down the stairway in a pile and land on top of PLUNKETT *at the foot of the stairs. The rest of the guests surge down towards the mêlée, all equally furious.*

INT. MAIN HALLWAY. NIGHT
PLUNKETT *picks himself up. The Americans look as if they could eat him alive.* JULIA *stirs in the wreckage of the suit of armour.*

PLUNKETT: As the brochure said – 'tis the unpredictability of spirits that cause problems. So I'd – eh – like to apologize for any minor inconvenience.
   (*Across a walkway behind him we see Miranda's bed whipping past out of control.*)

MALCOLM: This is the most pitiful supernatural sham I've ever encountered.
   (*Behind* MALCOLM *we see Miranda's bed flying down a spiral staircase.*)

PLUNKETT: But it will get better. I promise.
   (*Suddenly, from the corridor, Miranda's bed with* MIRANDA, BROTHER TONY *and* DAVEY *still on it, frozen with terror, flies towards* PLUNKETT, *drags him on to it and crashes into the nearby wall. No one can believe their eyes.*)

SHARON: That's it. We're leaving first thing in the morning.

PLUNKETT: Oh, no need for that! Just give the poor ghosts some time –

WOODY: We're history, dude.

PLUNKETT: Couldn't we look on tonight as a . . . kind of . . . dress rehearsal . . .

MALCOLM: You're finished, Plunkett. And I'm personally going to expose this pathetic fraud. There are laws against people like you.

KATIE: (*To* PLUNKETT) Maybe Jem Brogan'll give you another month.

(JACK *turns at the name, shocked.*)

JACK: What's Jem Brogan got to do with this?

KATIE: Jem Brogan holds the mortgage on this castle. We've got two weeks left before . . .

SHARON: (*Interrupting*) I'm very tired, Jack. Are you coming?

JACK: No, not yet. Go ahead, Plunkett.

PLUNKETT: So we told a lie. Everyone lies once in a while. So Katie isn't a ghost and Julia still has her head on and the castle isn't haunted. But what you've got to ask yourself is why did we do it? We did it because we love this place. (*He is bringing himself close to very theatrical tears.*) Every little worm-eaten brick. Every little nook and cranny. (*He really is crying now.*) Why should you Americans care if I lose my castle and the villagers lose their only means of employment?

JACK: I care.

PLUNKETT: What?

JACK: I'm involved in this. Jem Brogan is my father-in-law. (*The Irish all stop and stare at* JACK, *then at* SHARON.)

JULIA: You're Jem Brogan's daughter?

SHARON: Yes. My name is Brogan. And you might as well know there won't be any extensions on your mortgage. Especially after tonight's performance.

JACK: (*Aghast*) I don't believe this.

SHARON: Daddy asked me to check it out. (*To* PLUNKETT) That ghost business was too ridiculous.

PLUNKETT: So you came to sabotage us.

SHARON: You did perfectly fine all on your own. I didn't have to lift a finger. (*To* JACK) I'm going to bed. (*She strides up the stairs.* JACK *looks abjectly at* PLUNKETT.)

JACK: Look – I'm sorry. I didn't know. And for what it is worth, I think this place is great. (*The Irish stare at him in silence.* JACK *turns and runs up the stairs.*)

INT. CORRIDOR OUTSIDE JACK'S AND SHARON'S ROOM. NIGHT

JACK *catches up with* SHARON *in the corridor.* SHARON *whips around and turns on him.*

SHARON: Daddy wants this place. He's always wanted it. He was born in Haughlin. He hates the Plunketts.

JACK: Why?

SHARON: Why not? Daddy hates most people.

JACK: Jesus Christ, Sharon, you lied to me. You mean you used our vacation for 'Daddy'?

SHARON: Jack, it's business.

(JACK *can't believe what he's hearing.*)

Where are you going?

JACK: To get drunk.

SHARON: Stick to vodka. It won't smell so bad on your breath.

JACK: Don't worry. If I get drunk, I won't smell it!

(*He turns on his heels and stalks off.*)

INT. JACK'S AND SHARON'S ROOM. NIGHT

SHARON *briskly undresses by the window, only briefly exposing her beautiful body. Then she whips on her sleep mask and lies down like a mummy in the bed. We hear* JACK's *voice throughout.*

JACK: (*Voice over*) When I first met her, she had the most beautiful skin of any woman I'd ever met. It was white . . . that beautiful white . . . like . . .

PLUNKETT: Shaving cream?

INT. PUB. NIGHT

JACK *and* PLUNKETT *are drinking in the empty pub. They are both plastered.*

JACK: No – ala – ala something.

PLUNKETT: Ali? She had skin like Muhammad Ali?

(*They laugh drunkenly. There are tears in* JACK's *eyes.*)

Alka Seltzer?

(*They both crack up again.*)

Alaska. Baked Alaska.

JACK: No. I remember. Alabaster.

PLUNKETT: Oh dear. I knew a girl once.

JACK: White, translucent alabaster.

PLUNKETT: Yes. I knew a girl once.

JACK: Plunkett. I don't want you to lose your hotel. Not to my father-in-law. He's a son of a bitch.

PLUNKETT: Too kind. Far too kind. No, dear boy, he's a gobshite.

JACK: What's a gobshite?

PLUNKETT: Sorry. Far too kind. He's a whore's melt.

JACK: What's a whore's melt?

PLUNKETT: Part gobshite, part shitehawk, with a liberal sprinkling of godforsaken bollix thrown in.

JACK: Wow. He's bad.

PLUNKETT: What more could you expect of a man whose great, great grandfather was seen running down a boreen during the famine clutching a bowl of soup.

JACK: Soup, huh?

PLUNKETT: Whose grandmother was found under Biddy Coughlan's haystack clutching a rotten egg.

JACK: Wow. He's not only bad, he's a dickhead. So you knew a girl once?

PLUNKETT: Did I? Do you want a drink?

(JACK *holds up his whiskey. His words are now slurred.*)

JACK: I was under the impression that I had one.

PLUNKETT: I mean a real drink.

(PLUNKETT *ducks behind the bar. He pulls open a small door*

among the shelves – and we glimpse a row of old, dust-covered bottles inside.)
My father's brew.
(PLUNKETT *takes one out. Blows the dust off it. An opaque, cracked, mysterious bottle. He downs the liquid in one gulp.* JACK *does the same. It seems to twist his spine.)*
JACK: Wow! This isn't tap water.
PLUNKETT: What's he going to do with this place then?
JACK: How'd you like a view of the Pacific from the windows?
PLUNKETT: I don't believe you.
JACK: He's capable of it. Just look at his daughter.
　　(JACK *then breaks up. We don't know whether he's laughing or crying.* PLUNKETT *breaks up with him.)*
PLUNKETT: You mean your wife . . .
JACK: Omigod! You're right. I married her.
　　(They both drink again and break up laughing.)
PLUNKETT: No . . . don't laugh . . .
　　(They laugh to the point of tears.)
　　(Laughing) It could be . . . worse . . .
JACK: How?
PLUNKETT: *(Laughing)* It could be . . . *(He can barely get the words out, he's laughing so hard.)* Raining.

EXT. CASTLE. NIGHT
Rain teems down on the castle.

INT. CORRIDOR LOVE SEAT. NIGHT
JACK *wanders down the corridor taking swigs from the bottle of poteen. He is very drunk.*
JACK: Softness, Sharon. Just a little softness. Gentleness. A kiss here, a touch there. It's everything, Sharon. And it doesn't cost a thing.
　　(He comes to the door, tries to open it and finds it locked. He throws himself against it and falls through.)

INT. MARY'S BEDROOM. NIGHT
The room is in darkness. JACK *sways unsteadily.*
JACK: The milk of human kindness, Sharon. Three little words every once in a while. They don't cost anything either. I –

love – you. (*He sits on the bed. Then, realizes something.*)
Shit. Wrong room.
(*He senses something behind him. He turns and on the other
side of the bed sees a gravely beautiful girl, dressed in an
eighteenth-century nightgown – the girl from the portrait
downstairs –* MARY PLUNKETT.)
This isn't what you think.
(MARY *stares at* JACK. *Her eyes are luminous.*)
You're the girl in the painting downstairs, right?
Pretending to be a ghost?
(*Her eyes are hypnotic.* JACK *becomes entranced.*)
God, you're beautiful.
(*Suddenly, a huge wind rushes through the room. The door
bursts open and* MARTIN, *a fierce-looking man in an
eighteenth-century costume with a knife in his belt, rushes in.*
JACK *starts back in terror.*)

30

MARTIN: So, my little harlot, you'll not tup with me. Then
you'll tup with no one . . .
(MARTIN *drags* MARY *from the bed by her hair. He grabs her
round the neck and begins to strangle her.* JACK *sways
drunkenly above them.*)

JACK: Wow! Great act! Real bruises too. Should have done it
earlier. Could have saved this place.

MARTIN: Where is he?

MARY: No, Martin. No. Please!

MARTIN: I'll kill you, my precious wife. Then I'll kill him . . .
(MARTIN *drags* MARY *to her feet and flings her on to the bed.*)

JACK: Wait – that's a bit rough. Didn't anyone tell you the
show's over?

MARTIN: When I discover him.

MARY: Martin, there's no one. No one!

MARTIN: Then why don't I believe you?
(MARY *tries to rise.* MARTIN *suddenly plunges his sword in her
breast and this looks very real indeed.* MARY *slumps.*)
Oh Lord, she wouldn't die. Not with a lie on her lips.
What have I done?
(JACK *stares at her body, then turns to* MARTIN.)

31

JACK: You've killed her . . .
(*JACK rushes at* MARTIN, *as if to attack him. But* MARTIN *disappears, and* JACK *goes sprawling on the bed, over* MARY'S *body, which vanishes beneath him.*)
Oh, my God, no – (*He looks around the room, totally confused. Then he falls on the bed.*) Great act. Ten out of ten. (*He lies on the bed.*) Whoever you are, you're beautiful.
(*Then he senses something behind him again. He turns and sees* MARY *there exactly as before.*)
Jesus –

MARTIN: So, my little harlot, you'll not tup with me. Then you'll tup with no one –

MARY: No. Martin. No! Please –
(*And the scene is repeated exactly as before. Again,* JACK *is totally ignored.*)

JACK: Look, you two, please – can't you talk it out?
(*JACK lays his hand on* MARY's *arm. It passes right through.*)
Shit !!!
(*MARTIN unsheathes the huge sword.*)

MARY: Martin, there's no one. No one.

MARTIN: Then why don't I believe you?

JACK: Oh no! Don't kill her again –
(*MARTIN pulls back his arm, the sword glinting. Just as he's about to plunge it into* MARY, JACK *jumps between them and takes the sword in his heart. He screams. Magically, the sword passes right through him.* MARTIN *continues with the scene exactly as before, while* MARY *has been magically released from the loop.*)
My God – who are you –

MARY: Mary Plunkett.

JACK: What the hell is this?

MARTIN: Oh Lord, she wouldn't die. Not with a lie on her lips. What have I done?
(*He vanishes.* JACK *stares at* MARY *on the bed. She looks at him with infinite gratitude.*)

MARY: How can I thank you?

JACK: For what?

MARY: For your selflessness –

(*She leans forward as if to kiss him. As she does, her body is slowly vanishing.*)

JACK: I'm drunk. And you're the most beautiful – thing – I've ever –

(*Her body is vanishing, leaving just her beautiful head, the hair falling around it. Then her eyes and lips.*)

Oh God! Don't just go like that . . .

(*The last thing to go are her red lips, just as they reach his, in a kiss which seems to send shivers through him. A wind courses through his hair.*)

What is this –

(*The lips vanish.* JACK *stares round the empty room as if he is hallucinating.*)

INT. JACK'S AND SHARON'S ROOM. NIGHT

SHARON *is asleep.* JACK *breaks through the door and collapses beside her.*

JACK: Oh God, Sharon. You don't understand, do you? Why can't you just love me? I thought it would last forever. But it never even started. Did it, Sharon? Did you ever – love – me?

(SHARON *sleeps like a statue. Tears course down* JACK's *cheeks. He wipes them off.*)

The hell with it!

(*He staggers out of bed and into the bathroom. He rummages through Sharon's pills for the Valium. Then he fills a glass of water.*)

Better dead than half dead.

(*Behind him, we see the Valium tablets magically transposing themselves with the vitamins. We glimpse* MARY's *image in the mirror moving the pills.*)

Goodbye, Sharon.

(*He takes a handful of vitamins, sways and then collapses, thinking he has killed himself.*)

EXT. CASTLE. DAWN

Sun rising over the castle and village.

INT. JACK'S AND SHARON'S BATHROOM
A single beam of sunlight falls on JACK's *face, on the carpet.*
JACK: Dead. So this is what it feels like. Kind of like a
    hangover.
    (SHARON *enters and walks over him, as if he doesn't exist.*
    JACK *belches.*)
    You always hated me doing that, Sharon. But now that
    I'm dead, who cares? In fact, now that I'm dead I can tell
    you you've all the warmth of a penguin on an iceberg –
SHARON: And you smell like an explosion in a cut-rate
    brewery. Get up and pack.
JACK: Pack? You mean I'm not dead?
SHARON: No. But if I were you I wouldn't make any long-
    range plans. (*She goes over to the medicine cabinet, takes out
    her vitamin bottle.*) My vitamin B complex level is rock
    bottom and I can feel a massive migraine coming on.
JACK: No, Sharon – don't – (*She swallows a handful of pills and
    walks out of the door.*) Wrong pills . . .

INT. PLUNKETT'S OFFICE. MORNING
KATIE *enters, looking for* PLUNKETT, *but she can't find him
anywhere. Then she hears a groan coming from the roll-top desk.
She rolls back the top to reveal* PLUNKETT, *passed out from his
drink with* JACK.
KATIE: Mr Plunkett, wake up. Mrs Crawford has organized
    the Americans. They're leaving for Dublin after
    breakfast.
PLUNKETT: Oh, bloody hell!

INT. MAIN HALLWAY. MORNING
SHARON *is on the pay phone.*
SHARON: Daddy? It's me. You can forget about Plunkett. All
    the guests are coming to Dublin with me. So you'd better
    . . . (*Suddenly, the Valium kicks in. She starts giggling
    uncontrollably.*) You'd better get your – (*giggling, can
    hardly get the words out*) – get your fat ass over here –
    (*She falls against the wall and slumps to the floor, giggling, as*
    MALCOLM *comes in with his baggage.*)
    Get your fat ass over here and –

MALCOLM: You all right, Miss Crawford?
> (*She can't stop laughing. He bends to help her up, and as he does so, she kisses him on the mouth. Then she pulls away, abruptly and slaps him across the mouth.*)

SHARON: How dare you!
> (*She drops the phone and wanders down the corridor, zonked. The receiver of the phone begins to whip around of its own accord,* BROGAN's *voice coming from it.*)

BROGAN: Sharon? Sharon? What's wrong, honey? I'm coming over – next plane – I'm going to move that castle brick by brick to Malibu. Do you hear me, hon? Brick by brick –
> (*The receiver whirls towards the phone and replaces itself, shutting* BROGAN's *voice off.* MALCOLM *stares in amazement, rubbing his face.*)

INT. CORRIDOR LOVE SEAT. SAME TIME
JACK, *depressed, emerges from his room with his bags, and walks down the hallway. He comes to a love seat framed by windows. He sees the sun's rays coming through the window slowly forming the image of* MARY.
JACK: My God, you're real. I mean you're not. You're a real ghost . . .
> (*He goes to touch her face, but his hand sinks into her cheek.*)

INT. MAIN HALLWAY. SAME TIME
PLUNKETT *and* KATIE *watch all the Americans gather with their bags.*
KATIE: Maybe we should pray for rain.
PLUNKETT: You think that'll stop them?

INT. CORRIDOR OUTSIDE MRS PLUNKETT'S BEDROOM. DAY
A mysterious wind blows a chandelier. The camera tracks with it, as if we are assuming some ghostly point of view. We move through corridors of billowing curtains and tapestries, rattling light fixtures.

INT. MRS PLUNKETT'S BEDROOM. DAY
The camera homes in on Mrs Plunkett's door, and, as it does so, the door flies open, mysteriously, to reveal MRS PLUNKETT, *sitting at her table by the window, two drinks beside her. She turns and faces*

the camera.
MRS PLUNKETT: Good morning, dear.
  (*Reverse angle on the ghost of her husband,* PLUNKETT
  SENIOR. *A remarkably old gentleman, with bright intelligent
  eyes, wearing a satin dressing-gown, covered in dandruff.* MRS
  PLUNKETT *hands him his drink.*)
PLUNKETT SENIOR: Well, our son is an idiot.
MRS PLUNKETT: We've known that for years, darling.
PLUNKETT SENIOR: But this time he's surpassed himself. The
  ghosts are furious.
MRS PLUNKETT: Why?
PLUNKETT SENIOR: They've heard that Jem Brogan is going to
  move the castle to Malibu.
MRS PLUNKETT: Oooh, I'd like that. All that sunshine and those
  movie stars. Maybe I'd get to meet that J.R. fellow.
PLUNKETT SENIOR: No respectable ghost would move to
  California. They're Irish. What would they do there?
  They're outraged, and so am I. If that dolt knew how to
  maintain a proper castle, none of this would have happened.
MRS PLUNKETT: So what are we going to do?
PLUNKETT SENIOR: It's out of my hands. They won't listen to
  me. I'm afraid they're going to give the Americans the
  haunted holiday they came for.

INT. CORRIDOR LOVE SEAT. MOMENTS LATER
JACK, *with the ghost* MARY. *The ghost wind courses round them
intermittently.*
MARY: I have to thank you for what you did last night.
JACK: It was nothing. What did I do?
MARY: You gave me my first moment of peace in two hundred
  years. I'll be in your debt for eternity, sir.
JACK: I said it was nothing. And stop calling me sir.
MARY: What can I call you?
JACK: Jack.
MARY: Jack. Thank you, Sir Jack.
JACK: It's on me. (*He looks around, half confused, half
  embarrassed.*) Lovely dress.
MARY: My wedding dress. Today's my wedding day. Tonight
  he'll murder me.

37

JACK: You get murdered every night?

MARY: Every night until last night.

JACK: What about tonight?

MARY: That depends on you.

JACK: Why me?

MARY: Your love broke the chain – crossed the bound –

JACK: Omigod look – don't depend on me – my wife wouldn't understand –

MARY: Ah – 'twasn't love then –

JACK: Now I didn't say that either – it's just –

(*The horn blares outside.*)

I've go to go now.

(*The wind builds in strength.* JACK *rises slowly.* MARY *begins to fade.*)

40

MARY: Don't go, Jack . . .

JACK: Don't vanish –

MARY: But you want to forget me –

JACK: I don't know what I want! I only know you're –
> (*She vanishes entirely.*)
> You're the most beautiful thing I ever saw –
> (*The wind whips furiously. He claws the air.*)
> Shit –
> (*The wind drags him down the corridor.*)

EXT. CASTLE DRIVEWAY. DAY

The Americans sit piled in an ancient hearse. EAMON *is at the wheel,* WOODY *beside him.*

EAMON: So what did you have for breakfast this morning, sonny boy?

WOODY: Some damn fish.
> (SHARON *leans forwards and beeps the horn.*)

SHARON: JACK!!!
> (EAMON *starts the motor.*)

MONTAGE. VARIOUS PARTS OF THE CASTLE. DAY

A ghostly wind begins to gather out of every crevice of the castle, whipping into a fury.

INT. MAIN HALLWAY. DAY

JACK *reaches the staircase and begins to descend when the wind knocks him off his feet, and rips the suitcase from his hand. It whirls him down the staircase, out of the front door.*

EXT. CASTLE DRIVEWAY. DAY

JACK *flies past* KATIE *and over the Americans in the limousine.*

JACK: Waahooaahhoooooooahhhoooooo!!!
> JACK *flies out of sight, as the wind whirls round the limo, tearing it to bits. First, the luggage, piled on the roof, is sent flying. Then the limo itself is stripped by the force of the hurricane. Then the Americans are stripped naked.* BROTHER TONY *now wears only his clerical collar.* EAMON *is miraculously untouched. The wind vanishes, as quickly as it came. The Americans stare in horror at themselves.* SHARON,

41

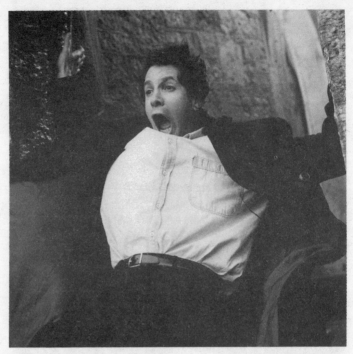

still stoned, looks down at BROTHER TONY's *naked body.*)
SHARON: So, all the snakes weren't driven out of Ireland.
   (BROTHER TONY *rips off his clerical collar and desperately
   tries to cover his crotch with it. It begins to pour. Thunder and
   lightning drive the naked Americans back to the castle.*)

EXT. CASTLE. DAY
JACK *is passed out in a tree, buffeted by the storm.*

INT. PLUNKETT'S OFFICE. DAY
PLUNKETT *is standing on a chair with the noose around his neck.*
PLUNKETT: '. . . Out, out, brief candle. Life's but a passing
   shadow, a poor player that . . .'
   (KATIE *bursts into the room.*)
KATIE: Mr Plunkett! The Americans are staying!
PLUNKETT: (*Raising his eyes to heaven*) There is a God!

EXT. CASTLE. MOMENTS LATER
JACK, *in the tree. He's dazed, but conscious. A bolt of lightning
strikes the trunk and the tree falls, tumbling* JACK *to the ground. A
ghostly white* HORSE *appears and stands above him, waiting.*
HORSE: Hi. Are you Jack?
   (JACK's *reaction.*)

EXT. CASTLE. DAY
*The Irish staff collect the Americans' clothes, which are scattered
all over the grounds.*

INT. MAIN HALLWAY. MOMENTS LATER
*The angry, drenched Americans are covering themselves in
whatever they can find.* MALCOLM *has wrapped some armour
round his waist;* BROTHER TONY *is now desperately trying to cover
his privates with a tapestry.* MIRANDA *is wearing the skimpiest
piece of chainmail while* SHARON *wanders around zonked in a
massive lamp shade.* PLUNKETT *bounces cheerily down the stairs.*
PLUNKETT: Welcome back, dear guests. Let me be the first to
   apologize for our temperamental Irish weather.
MALCOLM: Shut up, Plunkett, and call us a cab.
PLUNKETT: Of course, Mr Clay. Immediately. (*He tries the*

phone. He hangs up.) Deepest regrets. The phones are
dead. The storm must have knocked them out. Oh, darn!
I guess you'll just have to stay until it stops raining.
(*The rain suddenly stops. The sun shines brightly*.)
WOODY: Look, Dad. It's stopped raining.
PLUNKETT: (*Looking to the heavens*) Give me a break! Just one!
(*To the Americans*) So, we're all together for one more
night. I feel like we're all becoming one big, happy family.
MALCOLM: Plunkett, I would rather walk into town in this suit
of armour and spend the night in a stable than spend one
more second in this hellhole. Marge, children . . . we're
leaving.
(*The children groan.* MALCOLM *clanks in his makeshift suit
towards the door. As if on cue, the storm begins to rage again.
A bolt of lightning strikes* MALCOLM's *armour, illuminating
him. A rush of wind jets him up the stairs*.)
WENDY: (*Mouthing*) What the fuck was that?

EXT. CHAPEL. LATER
REYNALDO *the horse walks with* JACK *towards the chapel and
leads him inside*.

EXT. ROCKS BY LAKE. DAY
JACK *walks through the ruined interior and sees* MARY *materialize
by the altar. She is in her ghostly loop*.
MARY: Sweet Mother Mary, St Brigit, please don't let me
marry him. Please release me.
(JACK *reaches her. She doesn't seem to notice him*.)
JACK: Mary . . .
MARY: I don't love Martin and never will.
(*She still doesn't turn. The* HORSE *nuzzles* JACK.)
HORSE: Once more, with feeling –
JACK: (*Passionately*) MARY!!!
(MARY *turns.* JACK *is in a ragged state*.)
MARY: Sweet Jesus! What happened to you?
JACK: I ran into a puff of wind.
MARY: Oh dear. That would be the spirits in the castle. Sorry.
JACK: What are you doing?
MARY: Praying to St Brigit to release me from my marriage

vows. I'm to be . . .

JACK: I know. This is your wedding day and tonight you're
going to be murdered again. Look, this is too psychotic
for me. I mean, I'm as up for a good nervous breakdown
as anyone, but this is too much. I get here yesterday and
my marriage collapses. I save a ghost from being
murdered by another ghost, which, if you think about it,
makes no sense at all. Then, I fly into a tree and Reynaldo,
the talking horse here, leads me to . . .
(MARY *brings her face near his. Her eyes are luminous.*)
(*Almost swooning*) . . . the most beautiful ghost I've ever
seen in my . . . (*He shakes himself.*) I'm an American for
Christ's sake! What's going on here?

MARY: Last night, when you took Martin's sword in my stead,
you broke the cursed chain that has bound me for two
hundred years. Your heart. Your goodness.

JACK: What cursed chain?

MARY: My marriage to Martin Brogan was arranged by my
father. I did not love him. He had warts and his feet stank.
On my wedding night I refused to be tupped by him.

JACK: Tupped?

> (*She gives him a look.*)

Oh. Tupped. I get it. Go on.

MARY: He thought I loved another, though I did not. And in a jealous fury, he did me to death. Now every day for me is the same. If I get murdered one more time, I'll scream!

JACK: Jesus. Who'd be a ghost?

MARY: We are what we are.

> (*She blows his face again. It is incredibly sexy.*)

JACK: So, this Martin stank, did he?

MARY: Aye. And he squished.

JACK: Squished?

MARY: You know . . .

JACK: So you could love a man who belched . . . as long as he didn't squish.

MARY: I could love you, Sir Jack. And if you loved me, the miracle could happen.

JACK: But I can't. I'm married.

MARY: Ah, then. You don't love me.

JACK: I didn't say that . . .

MARY: And I am doomed forever. Even now, Martin dons his garments, sharpens his knife. Goodbye, Sir Jack.

> (*A magic wind begins to blow, wrapping a veil around* JACK.)

JACK: Wait. I didn't say that . . . (*He tries to pull the veil from her face.*) You're a ghost and I'm an American . . . it'd never work out.

> (*He can't see her anywhere. He is left holding the veil.*)

Come back . . . Mary . . .

> (*The veil turns to dust in his hands.*)

INT. JACK'S AND SHARON'S ROOM. SAME TIME

SHARON *is standing in a bath full of suds underneath an antique shower unit. Suddenly from the waters of the bath* MARTIN *emerges, surges upright standing behind her.* SHARON *doesn't notice.* MARTIN *belches loudly.*

SHARON: (*Out of shot*) Jack? Is that you?

> (MARTIN *belches again.*)

I don't know what happened to me, but I am zonked. I've got pains all over. Could you rub my back?

46

(MARTIN's *eyes widen, as* SHARON *turns languorously in the tub.*)
Go on. I won't bite.
(MARTIN *begins to rub her back.*)
(*Sniffing*) You could do with a bath. When did you last wash your feet?
(*And as* MARTIN's *hands ripple up and down her back, something amazing goes through her.*)
Oh God, Jack. You never did it like that before. Oh, honey . . . that's wonderful. Why don't you get in too?
(*She rolls over on her front.*)
MARTIN: (*Rolling his eyes to heaven*) Oh, Michael, Mary and all the saints. Oh, shitehawks McGoldrick.
(SHARON *pulls the washcloth away, sees* MARTIN *and screams.*)

INT. CORRIDOR OUTSIDE JACK'S AND SHARON'S ROOM. DAY
JACK *is running up the corridor when he hears* SHARON *scream.*

INT. JACK'S AND SHARON'S ROOM. DAY
He runs into his room and sees SHARON *standing cowering in the bathtub, a towel wrapped around her.*
SHARON: Oh, Jack! Oh, thank God you're here!
JACK: What is it?
SHARON: There was a terrible man here, watching me take a bath.
JACK: What did he look like?
SHARON: Warts – and big hands – and a knife –
JACK: (*Holding her*) It's OK. I'm here. That was only Martin.
SHARON: Martin? Who's Martin?
JACK: A ghost who murders his wife every night. Other than that, he's completely harmless.
SHARON: (*With rising hysteria*) Get out! Get out! Get out!

MARGE'S AND MALCOLM'S ROOM. DAY
MALCOLM *is lying in bed, his hair sticking out and his eyebrows singed.*
MARGE: Are you OK?
MALCOLM: Do I look OK?

47

(*He gets out of bed and starts assembling his paranormal equipment.*)

MARGE: What are you doing?

MALCOLM: I'm going to check this place out. I smell something wrong here.

MARGE: So do I. It smells like burnt rubber.

MALCOLM: That's me, Marge.

(*He exits with his equipment.*)

INT. CORRIDOR LOVE SEAT. MOMENTS LATER

JACK *walks down the hallway, towards the window seat where he met* MARY *earlier. He speaks to the empty seat.*

JACK: Talk to me, will you? You can't let him murder you again. Can't the two of you talk it out? I mean every couple has their problems.

(*A lace curtain by the window wraps itself around him.*)

Oh God. Yes. I mean no. I mean –

(PATRICIA *walks by, shaking her head, blessing herself.*)

PATRICIA: Crazy yanks . . .

INT. GALLERY. SAME TIME
MALCOLM *takes readings with his ghost-detecting paraphernalia. Suddenly, his equipment goes berserk. The needle rises upwards, pointing the finger at him. His Polaroid begins working of its own accord . . .*

INT. CLAY CHILDREN'S ROOM. DAY
The Clay children are staring open-mouthed at something.
WENDY: Do you believe this?
GRAHAM: No. Only four channels.
> (*They're looking at Irish television.* GRAHAM *goes back and forth through the four channels – getting test patterns, a cricket match, and an aerobics programme.*)
WOODY: Maybe the cable got unplugged.
WENDY: Nope. No cable. This is it.
GRAHAM: This place sucks the big one.
> (*He picks up a book and flings it at the television set.*)
WENDY: Graham!
> (*The book heads for the screen, and goes into it and is flung back by the woman inside.*)
GRAHAM: Holy moly . . .
> (*The book suddenly flies back – right at* WOODY. GRAHAM *grabs his sister and jerks her out of the way. The book flies around the room, pages whirling everywhere.* WENDY *screams, falling to the floor. Above her, a candleholder comes to life. The candleholders fly down and pinion her to the carpet, like carnival knives. The other children scream in terror, staring at her. A chest of drawers begins to shudder across the room. The drawers fly out like arrows towards the children who fling themselves to the floor. The drawers fly into the walls, TV etc., leaving the room in chaos. A beat of silence. Then, the door opens. The kids stare in silent terror – but see* KATIE *peering in.* KATIE *looks aghast at the destruction of the bedroom.*)
KATIE: You little pack of American heathens!
KIDS: We didn't do anything. We swear!

INT. CORRIDOR OUTSIDE MRS PLUNKETT'S BEDROOM.
SAME TIME
JACK *wanders down, still talking to himself.*
JACK: Can't we just take one step at a time? I mean eternity's a
    big commitment and –
    (*The door to* MRS PLUNKETT's *room opens, and he sees her
    inside.*)
MRS PLUNKETT: You do love her, don't you?
JACK: Yes . . . but . . .
MRS PLUNKETT: What's the problem then?
JACK: Well, she's a ghost. (*Puzzled*) How do you know all this?
MRS PLUNKETT: I'm married to one. Won't you join us for a
    drink?

INT. BROTHER TONY'S ROOM. SAME TIME
BROTHER TONY *is praying by the window. His head bowed.*
BROTHER TONY: Dear Lord, I beseech thee to help me in my
    hour of need. Cleanse me of the impure thoughts I have
    for this woman, Miranda.
    (*He looks up. Across the courtyard, he sees* MIRANDA *dancing
    erotically to Madonna's 'Poppa don't preach'.*)
    Well now, Lord. That's not quite the kind of help I had in
    mind.
    (*Abruptly, he hears the flapping of wings and turns to see
    empty nuns' habits flying about the room. 'Poppa don't
    preach' changes to a threatening 'Dies irae'. The habits attack
    him, shrieking and pecking like the crows from Hitchcock's*
    The Birds. BROTHER TONY *looks down and sees smoke
    coming out of his pants pockets.*)
    Oh Lord, I get the message.
    (*Then the habits swoop towards him all at once. He panics
    and dives out the window, right into the slime-covered
    swimming pool.*)

INT. MIRANDA'S ROOM. SAME TIME
MIRANDA *hears the sounds of terror from Brother Tony's room. She
rushes to the door.*

INT. BROTHER TONY'S ROOM. SAME TIME
MIRANDA *bursts in. She sees the empty room.*
MIRANDA: Tony? Brother Tony?
   (*She closes the door behind her. We see the nuns' habits behind
   her, waiting ominously.*)
   What the hell –
   (*As she moves to the window, she hears the rustle of cloth. She
   turns, sees the leering nuns' habits and screams. They whip
   towards her, like demons, and wrap themselves round her
   body, lifting her in the air. They drag her towards the
   window, and through it.*)

EXT. POOL. SAME TIME
BROTHER TONY *struggles in the slimy water, fish crawling in his
hair.* MIRANDA *falls straight into his arms, dumped from above.*

INT. MRS PLUNKETT'S BEDROOM. LATER
JACK *and* MRS PLUNKETT *are drinking.*
JACK: How can it possibly work out? She's a ghost . . . Not to
   mention the fact that we're both married to other people.
MRS PLUNKETT: True love can move mountains.
JACK: It can't bring the dead back to life.
MRS PLUNKETT: It can . . . on All-Hallows.

JACK: That's tomorrow night.

MRS PLUNKETT: Yes. When true love will let the spirit take on the flesh. When the spirit moves and the flesh is willing. When the juices flow and the skelping is mighty.

JACK: Skelping?

MRS PLUNKETT: A ghost term. (*Dreamily*) Best night of the year.

JACK: You're serious.

MRS PLUNKETT: Of course. But it's dangerous. You mustn't go too far!

JACK: What do you mean?

(MRS PLUNKETT *cocks her eye towards the wardrobe.*)

MRS PLUNKETT: Shall we help him, dear?

(*The wardrobe creaks open, revealing a dusty book on a shelf. It moves of its own accord towards* JACK, *right into his hands.*)

The Book of High Spirits. You'll find all you need to know in there.

(JACK *blows the dust off the book*.)

JACK: Thank you.

MRS PLUNKETT: Don't mention it. Just promise you'll be careful.

EXT. CASTLE. NIGHT

A full moon appears from behind a cloud, casting its light over the castle. The strains of La Bohème *drift across the lake.*

INT. DINING ROOM. NIGHT

All the Americans are huddled in the bar. PLUNKETT *enters and they all leap, as if expecting the worst. They sigh with relief when they see it is* PLUNKETT.

MARGE: Oh, it's only you.

PLUNKETT: Who did you think it was?

MALCOLM: Come off it, Plunkett. Those fake ghosts were one thing, but this carry on is entirely different.

PLUNKETT: Is there something wrong with your rooms?

AMERICANS: (*One voice*) THEY'RE HAUNTED!!!

PLUNKETT: Well, the brochure did promise –

MALCOLM: Damn the brochure! We're talking real live spirits here. How do you explain that, Plunkett?

(*He holds up his broken ectoplasmeter.*)

PLUNKETT: The weather?

SHARON: (*Standing up*) Oh, come off it. Don't you see what he's doing? He wants to keep us here. It's the only way he can hang on to this dump. I don't know about the rest of you, but, Plunkett, you haven't fooled me at all.

(*She exits.* PLUNKETT *whispers to* KATIE.)

PLUNKETT: (*Sotto voce*) These Americans are becoming a gigantic pain in the arse. (*To the Americans*) Personally, I've found the best pookha repellent to be a glass of poteen. So if anyone cares to join me . . .

AMERICANS: Yes – please – just don't leave us!

(*He walks to the bar, with the Americans in a bunch behind him.*)

INT. MARY'S ROOM. NIGHT

JACK *is reading the* The Book of High Spirits.

53

JACK: 'On All-Hallows, the dead take flesh, wrap their limbs about the living and feed on human fear of them. Ghost and human may conjoin, they may skelp but not tup for should a man bed a ghostly body, untold demons shall be loosed upon the world.'

(JACK *hears the door open.*)

Mary?

(*It's* SHARON.)

SHARON: Who's Mary?

JACK: Sharon, we've got to talk.

SHARON: Who is this Mary?

JACK: She's a woman. Actually, she's not a woman. She's a ghost. But it's funny how much you can care about a ghost and I think I'm . . . (*Looking down at the book again*) Have you ever heard of skelping?

SHARON: Stop! Don't you sit there and tell me you're having an affair with a goddamn ghost!

JACK: It's true, Sharon.

SHARON: There's no such thing as ghosts.

(*Suddenly, the window is thrown open and wind swirls around the room.* MARY *appears, pursued by* MARTIN, *who proceeds to try and strangle her in a perfect replay of the night before.*)

That was the man in the bathroom!

JACK: That's Martin and Mary. They're ghosts. They're having problems in their relationship.

(MARTIN *throws* MARY *on the bed.*)

MARY: No, Martin. Please.

MARTIN: I'll kill you, my precious wife. Then I'll kill him. When I discover him.

(*He draws his knife.* JACK *tries to stop him, but* SHARON *drags him back.*)

MARY: Martin, there's no one.

SHARON: Oh yes there is! My husband!

MARTIN: (*To* MARY) Then why don't I believe you?

(*He goes for the kill.*)

SHARON: Believe this.

(*She gives him a karate chop to the groin, her foot travels through him upending her on the floor at his feet.* MARTIN

looks down at her thunderstruck, as MARY *runs out of the door.* MARTIN *has fallen out of the loop.*)

INT. CORRIDOR LOVE SEAT. NIGHT
MARY *runs down the hallway.*
JACK: Mary . . . wait!
　　(*She turns.*)
　　Don't go. Listen to me. I love you.
MARY: I know that.
JACK: When did you know it?
MARY: The minute I saw you. The minute I knew I loved you.
　　(*She comes towards him.*)
　　But your love must be true.
JACK: It is true.
MARY: It must withstand all obstacles.
JACK: It will! It will! I've been reading . . . By the way, what's
　　skelping?
MARY: This is skelping.
　　(*She comes towards him, wraps herself around him, and does*

something erotic. The wind courses through JACK's *hair. He is in ecstasy.*)

JACK: Oh, my God!
　　(*He sees* MARY *begin to vanish.*)
　　Don't go, Mary!
MARY: I can't help it. Skelping takes a lot out of you.
　　(*She is almost gone.*)
　　Just remember I love you.
JACK: I love you.
MARY: Then meet me in my chambers. Midnight tomorrow.
　　(*She vanishes.* JACK *is left with the wind.*)

INT. MARY'S ROOM. SAME TIME
MARTIN *is writhing on the floor, clutching his groin.*
MARTIN: That was a dirty trick . . . right in the bahokkies!
SHARON: You were going to put a sword through your wife, you pig!
MARTIN: It's no great thing. I do it every night.
SHARON: And I suppose watching other men's wives take a bath is no big deal either.
MARTIN: It's a grand thing if the wife is you.
SHARON: You dirty Peeping Tom!
　　(*He begins to vanish. He reaches for her.*)
MARTIN: One skelp before I vanish . . .
　　(SHARON *goes to kick him again.*)
　　(*As he disappears*) Not again, my wild vixen. But God, what a woman you are!
　　(*He is gone.* SHARON *looks almost regretful.*)
SHARON: You're not so bad yourself.

INT. ENTRANCE HALL. NIGHT
PLUNKETT *descends the stairs wearily. His staff are gathered below.*
PLUNKETT: So what's wrong with them, eh? What's wrong with these Americans? One night they want to leave, the next night you can't get rid of them. One day they hate the whiting, next day they have to have all five courses. When you break your back to give them ghosts you thought they wanted, they scream at you. And when you throw in the

56

towel, they scream even louder. They see spooks in the toilet. Under the bed. I mean, don't they know when the joke's over? Can't they tell when enough is enough? (*The wall behind him slowly melts, revealing the family crypt, where his dead ancestors lie on their catafalques, covered in the dust of centuries. They slowly come to life and move towards him. Old uncles, with purple faces, goitred aunts, babies who died at birth, grandfathers, grandmothers, great-grandmothers. The Irish stare in terror from* PLUNKETT *to the display behind them.* PLUNKETT *screams.*) Will somebody say something! WHAT IS WRONG WITH THEM – WHAT IS GOING ON HERE?!

EAMON: Eh, Mr Plunkett – I think someone wants a word –

PLUNKETT: Who?

EAMON: Your great-uncle Peter and your great-aunt Nan and granny Joyce and her half-sister, not to mention – (*The final ghost comes down the centre of the staircase. It is*

PLUNKETT SENIOR, *for whom the other ghouls make way.*)
Your father –
(PLUNKETT *freezes. He whispers.*)
PLUNKETT: But he's dead –
EAMON: I know. And he looks pretty angry too –
PLUNKETT SENIOR: And I have every right to be.
PLUNKETT: (*Turning*) Father!
PLUNKETT SENIOR: Considering what you've done with our
    ancestral home.
(PLUNKETT *screams in terror at the ghoulish display of his
ancestors, who suddenly whirl into gleeful activity, surging
towards the Irish, terrifying them out of their lives.*)

INT. OFFICE. SAME TIME
The door crashes open and PLUNKETT *falls through, slamming it
behind him.*
PLUNKETT SENIOR: (*Out of shot*) Did you really think you
    could get away from me?
(PLUNKETT *whirls around to see his father already in the
room. In the background we can hear the screams of the Irish
staff being pursued by the ghosts.*)
PLUNKETT: Leave me alone. You're dead –
PLUNKETT SENIOR: Not so dead that I can't see what a
    numbskull you are.
PLUNKETT: Oh, fine. Call me names. That's so easy.
PLUNKETT SENIOR: Peter, Peter, what have you done with
    yourself???
PLUNKETT: What did you have to leave me this place for? You
    knew I was an incompetent. All I wanted to be was a
    happy drunk. You made me a miserable one, leaving me
    this place, staff to run, bills to be paid . . . Then dying on
    me. Just like that! Most people give some warning, you
    know, premature senility, angina, gout – bed-ridden for
    years. But not you – healthy as an old goat, you pop off
    one day in the orchard, and what then? Not a goddamn
    word. Not a whisper. Didn't it ever occur to you that I
    might need some advice – that I might miss you?
(*Tears in* PLUNKETT SENIOR's *eyes. He places his hand on
his son's shoulder. It sinks in.*)

PLUNKETT SENIOR: Peter, I never thought . . .
 (*Now* PLUNKETT *is crying too.*)
PLUNKETT: It's true, you old goat. I missed you. You're the
 only –
PLUNKETT SENIOR: Give your daddy a hug.
 (PLUNKETT *goes tearfully to hug his father, but falls through
 and crashes down on the floor.*)
 Sorry, Peter.

EXT. CASTLE. DAWN
The castle, surrounded by early morning mist.

INT. KITCHEN. DAY
SAMPSON *and* PATRICIA *preparing dinner.* MALCOLM *comes in.*
MALCOLM: Remember, if you see anything, ignore it. Ignore it
 totally. Pretend you didn't see it. Got it?
SAMPSON: Got it.
 (*One of the whiting* SAMPSON *is preparing begins to whistle
 loudly.* SAMPSON *quickly chops his head off.*)
 It didn't even happen, did it?
PATRICIA: Nope.
SAMPSON: Don't you just love whiting?

INT. JACK'S AND SHARON'S ROOM. DAY
SHARON *is sitting on her bed, filing her nails, when* MARTIN
appears.
MARTIN: Madame, for you I've missed my wedding for the
 first time in years. That's how much I want ye.
 (SHARON *stares at him haughtily.*)
 Now it's true I'm a ghost and a murderer. But forgetting
 all that, tonight is All-Hallows, one night in the year I
 become flesh. What say ye to a bit of skelping?
 (SHARON *turns her head away and ignores him.*)
 At least tell me your name.
 (*He begins to disappear from the head downwards. All that is
 left is a pair of legs and a groin.* SHARON *turns and takes a
 peek.*)
SHARON: Wow!
 (MARTIN *begins to appear again, head and torso.*)

MARTIN: Madame, I've the best balhookie from here to
    Muckinderry. What say you we give it a whirl?
SHARON: Drop dead.
MARTIN: (*Smitten*) What a woman!
    (*She turns away again and ignores him. The rest of* MARTIN
    vanishes.)

EXT. CASTLE. EVENING
*The castle, seen from across the lake, the wishing tree in the
foreground. As the light fades, small sputtering lights begin to emerge
from the murky waters of the bog, like fireflies. They whiz about,
making strange ghostly sounds as if talking to one another.*

INT. JACK'S AND SHARON'S ROOM. NIGHT
JACK *is having a bath, preparing himself for his date with* MARY.
The Book of High Spirits *is propped up beside him. He reads, as if
it were a sex manual.*
JACK: 'He who tups the pure spirit finds only the grave.' (*Shakes
    his head.*) 'But even in the grave, true love conquers all.'

INT. PUB. NIGHT
Everyone is getting drunk.
SAMPSON: Don't ghosts like whiskey?
MALCOLM: Only Irish ones.
    (*On the stage, with its quaint image of coconut trees, etc., a
    cardboard cloud moves across the cardboard sun. Nobody
    notices.*)
    Look, the whole thing may have been no more than a local
    disturbance in the extra-planer ether. A kind of
    supernatural burp if you see what I mean.
    (MALCOLM's *hair is being blown and droplets of spray hit his
    face. He looks at the stage and sees a 'painted' storm building up
    on it, and cardboard waves moving boats, blowing across
    it . . .*)
    Ah – Davey, another drink . . .
    (*The 'storm' builds on the stage, whipping the coconuts off the
    cardboard trees. Real coconuts fly through the pub, with huge
    gusts of wind now, washes of water, seaweed, real fish. The
    humans stare in terror.*)

(*Hissing*) Rubbish – ignore it – pathetic show – (*He dodges a coconut.*) Davey – quick – drinks all round –
(*A wave washes over him, throwing him against the bar.*)

INT. JACK'S AND SHARON'S ROOM. NIGHT
JACK *stands before a mirror, smoothing his hair.*
JACK: (*Singing*) Chances are, my composure sort of slips.
  The moment you come into view . . .
  (*He strikes one final suave pose and exits, turning out the light.*)

INT. PUB. NIGHT
Everyone drinking at the bar, and, in their efforts to ignore the apparitions, displaying a rare camaraderie. MALCOLM *is attempting a pathetic brogue, as the wind and waves whip around them.*
MALCOLM: Confidentially, boyos, *entre nous*, if I may go
  French for a sec., I've never seen a ghost till I came to the auld sod.
  (*On the painted sea an 'island' spouts paper; water moves, and a head emerges, revealing itself to be a whale.*)
  (*Looking at whale*) I've exposed every fake in the book though . . .
  (*A whale's tail whips through the pub and knocks him to the ground.*)

INT. MARY'S ROOM. NIGHT
The room is empty, but beautifully lit by the candelabra. A soft breeze comes through the windows. JACK *places the champagne on a side table, sits by the bed and waits.* MARY, *still a ghost, enters, wearing her wedding gown.*
MARY: (*Shyly*) Hello.
JACK: Hello.
  (*The village bells begin to toll midnight. On each stroke,* MARY *becomes less of a ghost and more of a woman. By the final bell, she's fully flesh. A beat while they take each other in.* JACK *holds his hand out and they touch for the first time. Then, they kiss. The door opens and* PLUNKETT *looks through.* MARY *breaks the kiss.*)

PLUNKETT: Good God, it's my great-great-great-great-great
     grandmother.
MARY: Hello.
PLUNKETT: Can I get you anything? After all these years –
JACK: Well, we – ah –
PLUNKETT: Oh. (*He winks broadly.*) Oh, my goodness – how
     wonderful . . . I'm terribly happy for you both.
     (*He leaves.* MARY *brings her lips again to* JACK's.)

INT. CRYPT. NIGHT
The midnight bell echoes through the crypt, awaking Plunkett's
ghostly ancestors. PLUNKETT *himself sticks his head in, like a*
genial host.
PLUNKETT: Everybody comfortable? Happy? Anything I can
     get you? Drinks?
     (*The ancestors grin.*)
UNCLE PETER: Mine's a large one –
GREAT-AUNT NAN: Rum and black.
GREAT-GRANNY PLUNKETT: A Delemaine brandy, boy, with a
     dash of soda –

INT. PUB. NIGHT
MALCOLM *picks himself up from the seaweed-covered ground.*
MARGE: You poor dear –
MALCOLM: It's nothing, Marge. Ignore it.
MARGE: (*Staring at the stage*) It's looking at us.
     (*Through the moving card waves we see a periscope emerging,*
     then a submarine, like the Nautilus, *with a giant squid*
     clinging to the conning tower.)
     (*In terror*) Malcolm –
MALCOLM: It's not happening, ignore it – it's a bad dream –
     (*Great tentacles from the squid whip through the pub,*
     wrapping round MARGE. *She screams.*)
MARGE: I can't ignore it –
     (MARGE *struggles. Three of the tentacles wrap round* WOODY,
     dragging him towards the stage. MARGE *tries to pull him*
     back.)
     Woody, my God, help me –
     (*But* WOODY *is whipped out of sight.* MARGE *wails*

62

hysterically, seeing: a tiny cardboard cutout of WOODY, *waving in fear, wrapped in the squid's arms, which is vanishing beneath the cardboard waves.*)

INT. MARY'S ROOM. MOMENTS LATER
JACK *and* MARY *are still engrossed in the kiss which seems to last for ever.*
MARY: My God!
JACK: I know.
MARY: I've never felt anything quite like that.
JACK: I have. Lots of times.
MARY: You have?
JACK: No. That was just a kind of twentieth-century American joke.

INT. PUB. NIGHT
The cardboard seascape. WOODY *vanishes and disappears beneath different sets of waves. In the pub,* MARGE *grabs a lifebuoy, fixed to the wall. She throws it towards the stage. On the stage: a tiny cardboard lifebuoy sails towards the cardboard* WOODY. *He grabs it. In the pub:* MARGE *and everyone pulls on the rope. On the stage:* WOODY *grabs the rope. A tug of war begins, from the pub to stage. The entourage hauls on the rope, as does the cardboard squid, the*

hapless cardboard WOODY *caught between them. Then, just when he seems about to be dragged for ever beneath the waves, a massive ocean liner steams into view, crushing the submarine and the squid beneath it.* WOODY *is released, dragged through the air on the rope. In the pub: everyone hauling on the rope collapses on the floor.* WOODY *flies through the air and lands on top of them, drenched and terrified.*

MARGE: My poor baby –

> (*She embraces him.* PLUNKETT *enters, looks bemusedly at everyone on the sodden floor.*)

PLUNKETT: Having fun?

MALCOLM: This is your fault, Plunkett –

PLUNKETT: (*Beaming*) Yes, all my own work –

> (*On the stage, the foghorn of the liner blares. A walkway drops down and disgorges its ghostly passengers – Plunkett's ancestors, all looking for their drinks.*)

GREAT-GRANNY PLUNKETT: Where's that bloody brandy, boy?

UNCLE PETER: Typical!

GREAT-AUNT NAN: Call this a hotel?

> (PLUNKETT *runs in confusion to the bar.*)

PLUNKETT: Drinks, Davey!

> (MALCOLM *grabs him.*)

MALCOLM: No, you idiot! Ignore them.

PLUNKETT: How?

MALCOLM: Think of something –

PLUNKETT: Katie – a song –

MIRANDA: Yes, that one with twenty verses –

> (KATIE *begins to sing an interminable ballad. Everyone pretends to love it – ignoring the ghosts, who cover their ears in anguish.*)

UNCLE PETER: *Boring!!!*

> (*He walks into a shadow and vanishes. The other ancestors follow . . .*)

INT. MARY'S ROOM. NIGHT

JACK *kissing* MARY. MARY *breaks the kiss.*

MARY: Remember, Sir Jack. The line we cannot cross.

JACK: Mmmm. You call this a tup?

(*He kisses her again.*)

MARY: No. But it's not too far off . . .

JACK: Mmmmm.

    (*They break away with great difficulty.*)

    Champagne! Nothing like champagne to take our minds off you-know-what.

    (*He pops the cork, pours two glasses and hands her one.*)

MARY: Drink to me only with thine eyes

    And I will pledge with mine.

    Or leave a kiss within the cup

    And I'll not ask for wine.

JACK: That's so beautiful. Who wrote it?

MARY: Ben Jonson.

    (*They toast and stare into one another's eyes.*)

JACK: Funny. I can't think of anything except you-know-what.

MARY: Sing something.

JACK: What?

MARY: Anything. To keep our minds off . . .

JACK: You-know-what.

    (*He raises his glass.*)

    There ain't nothing in the world

    Like a big-eyed girl

    To make me act so funny.

    Make me spend my money

    Make me feel real loose

    Like a long-necked goose

    Like a duck.

    Oh, baby. That a-what I like.

MARY: Who wrote that?

JACK: The Big Bopper.

INT. PUB. NIGHT

KATIE *is singing the last verse of her interminable song. The last ghosts are fading. The stage is as it always was. She finishes, and there is a beat of silence, of utter normality. Then* KATIE *whoops.*

KATIE: We did it!!!

INT. MARY'S ROOM. NIGHT

JACK *and* MARY *inch towards the four-poster bed, kissing all the while.* MARY *bolts up.*

MARY: No more, Jack. No more.

JACK: You're right. This is all wrong. I'm married. You're married. You're a ghost. I'm not. It can't work. Let's just be friends. OK?

MARY: Agreed.

(*They shake hands – then instantly fall on each other once more.*)

INT. MAIN HALLWAY. NIGHT

MALCOLM *walks stealthily through the empty castle with his ectoplasmeter. It is as quiet as a grave. The whole entourage follows. He comes to the massive front doors. He opens them with a frightening creak.*

EXT. CASTLE. NIGHT

A wonderfully full moon illuminates the lawns. One by one, the humans emerge from the castle, as if they cannot believe the peace and quiet. They walk slowly towards the castle gates.

INT. MARY'S ROOM. NIGHT

MARY *and* JACK *are naked under a sheet.*

JACK: My God, are all ghosts like this?

MARY: Are all balhookies like yours?

EXT. LAKE. NIGHT

The entire group stands on a hill overlooking the castle. They wait. Nothing. MIRANDA *whispers to* BROTHER TONY.

MIRANDA: It really is beautiful –

BROTHER TONY: Not as beautiful as you.

MALCOLM: We may have won . . .

(PLUNKETT *takes out a flask and passes it to* MALCOLM.)

INT. MARY'S ROOM. NIGHT

JACK *and* MARY *are making love.*

MARY: Oh God, Jack! Yes! I mean no!

EXT. LAKE. NIGHT

The entire group stand with their backs to the bog-hole into which the bus tumbled. There is not a ghost in sight.

MALCOLM: I formally declare this a spirit-free zone.

  (*They break into wild cheers and embraces.*)

SHARON: Don't you just love this country?

INT. MARY'S ROOM. SAME TIME

MARY: Oh God, Jack. We can't. We mustn't. There, there.
  Touch me there. Faster. Now slower. Now, stop! It's not
  right. Don't stop. There, there. Touch me there. Faster.
  Now, slower. Now, stop. Remember our promise. Oh
  God, Jack, tup me. Tup me.

JACK: I'm tupping, I'm tupping.

EXT. LAKE. NIGHT

Something emerging now from the slimy waters of the bog.
Something metallic, infinitely horrible.

INT. MARY'S ROOM. NIGHT

More passion.

MARY: Tup me more!

JACK: Like that?

MARY: Oh God! Yes!

EXT. LAKE. NIGHT

Something rising caused by the union of human and ghost in the
castle. We see now it is the bus, covered in slime, rising to a height
of several feet above the bog water. None of the humans has
noticed.

MALCOLM: Of course, if one of us – even one of us – had
  acknowledged the existence of those things, in any way,
  we would have blown the whole shebang.

  (*The bus rises even higher behind them.* PLUNKETT *turns. He*
  sees the bus and beams with delight.)

PLUNKETT: Ah . . . perfect . . .

  (*We see, through the slime-covered windows, every loathsome*
  apparition we have seen to date. MARTIN, *Mary's ghost*
  husband, is at the wheel, grinning lustfully at SHARON. *He*
  shouts.)

MARTIN: Sharon. I love thee!

67

SHARON: (*Turning*) Oh, Jesus! Oh, God!
MARTIN: It's the hour of the balhookie.
　　　(*The entire entourage turns, sees the bus, and freezes in terror.*)

INT. MARY'S ROOM. NIGHT
MARY: Oh, Jack. I love you!
　　　(JACK *and* MARY *seem to be devouring each other.*)
JACK: I love you. I love you.
　　　(*Then, both seem to explode.*)

EXT. LAKE. NIGHT
The phantoms pour out from every orifice of the bus, crashing through windows, exhaust pipes and doors. They are demonic, powerful, terrifying. The humans scream in terror and scatter in all directions. REYNALDO, *the horse, rears and hoots with glee.*

INT. MARY'S ROOM. NIGHT
MARY *seems suddenly spent in* JACK's *arms. He touches her face.*
MARY: Jack, Jack, we shouldn't have . . .
　　(*Something is happening to her skin.* JACK *doesn't see.*)
JACK: Mary. My God, that was something . . .
　　(*Suddenly,* JACK *sees that* MARY *has begun to age. He withdraws his hand in horror.*)
　　What's happening, Mary?
MARY: Jack, it's the Powers. I'm two hundred years old.
　　(*And she becomes it, before our very eyes. A two-hundred-year-old corpse.*)
JACK: (*In horror*) 'He who tups with pure spirit tups the grave.'
　　(JACK *leaps away from her in terror. He grabs his clothes. She moans at him pitifully.*)
MARY: Jack, don't leave me!

EXT. LAKE. NIGHT
MARTIN *drives the ghost-laden bus through the crowd of humans,*
heading for SHARON.
MARTIN: Oh, my beauty. My beauty . . .

INT. SPIRAL STAIRCASE. NIGHT
JACK *flees through the corridor, pursued by Mary's corpse.*
MARY: Just tell me you love me, Jack. Make it all right . . .
JACK: You're a corpse. You're not Mary. Get away from me.

INT./EXT. MAIN HALLWAY/ CASTLE. NIGHT
The nose of the bus crashes into the castle wall. MARTIN *is*
propelled out of the driver's seat, slams through the window and
crashes into JACK *who is running down the staircase, fleeing from*
MARY. JACK *tries to disentangle himself.*
MARTIN: Where's the wife?
> (JACK *points at* MARY's *corpse at the top of the stairs.*)
> Not mine, you dolt! Yours.
> (*He sees* SHARON *running through the hallway below.*)
> My beauty.
> (*He pursues her.* JACK *turns and sees* MARY's *corpse*
> *advancing. He runs down the stairs away from it.*)

70

INT. MAIN HALLWAY AND DINING ROOM. NIGHT
JACK *rushes into the dining room and slams the door behind him.
He bumps into* SHARON, *who is cowering behind it. She screams –
then sees it is* JACK *and seems almost disappointed.*
SHARON: Oh. It's only you.
JACK: Only? Who did you expect?
SHARON: Oh, shut up!
    (MARTIN *appears behind her.*)
MARTIN: My beauty . . .
    (*He grabs her.* SHARON *breaks free of him and, as if enjoying
    the chase, makes for the door. She pulls it open.* MARY'S
    corpse falls in on top of her.*)
MARY'S CORPSE: Jack – Jack – Say something.
SHARON: Oh, my God! Oh, my God! That's what you've been
    having an affair with. You threw me over for her?
JACK: Well, at least she said she loved me. More than you ever
    did.
MARY'S CORPSE: I do love you, Jack.
    (MARTIN *draws his knife in fury, falling into his old jealous
    role.*)
MARTIN: I'll kill you, my precious wife. Then I'll kill him.
JACK: Look, don't start that again.
MARTIN: Unfaithful wretch.
    (*He raises the knife.* SHARON *gives him another black-belt
    karate chop, sending the knife flying across the room.*)
SHARON: She looks dead enough already.
MARTIN: (*To* JACK) Your wife is quite a person.
JACK: So is yours.
    (*He looks at* MARY'S *corpse.*) So was yours.
SHARON: You were made for each other.
MARTIN: As we were –
    (*He embraces her dramatically. She breaks away giggling.*)
SHARON: (*Giggling*) Stop it, you great big brute, you!!!
MARTIN: Come, my little tupstress –
    (*He chases* SHARON *out. She seems to want to be caught.*)
    Goodbye, Mary! Forgive me for the last two hundred
    years!
    (*Silence.* JACK *looks sadly at* MARY'S *corpse.*)

MARY'S CORPSE: You said you'd love me for ever.
JACK: You were different then.
MARY'S CORPSE: Only on the outside. Inside, I'm the same.
JACK: I know looks aren't everything . . .
MARY'S CORPSE: I'm here Jack – kiss me –
JACK: But they can be a help –
MARY'S CORPSE: Kiss me, Jack – one last time.
　　(*She moves close to* JACK. *He grimaces and closes his eyes.*)
JACK: Just once, now –

INT. CORRIDOR OUTSIDE MARY'S ROOM. NIGHT
SHARON, *laughing and freer than we have ever seen her, runs
through the corridor. We hear* MARTIN'S *voice.*
MARTIN: Be with me, love. For ever.
SHARON: Sure.
　　(*She stops. A wind whips round her, but there is no sign of*
　　MARTIN.)
　　Where the hell are you?
　　(*The door of Mary's room is open. She walks towards it.*)

INT. MAIN HALLWAY. NIGHT
JACK's *lips, meeting those of the corpse. She is changing back,
through the kiss.* JACK's *eyes are still closed.*

INT. MARY'S ROOM. PRE-DAWN
SHARON, *in the darkened room. She sees* MARTIN *standing by the
open window.*
MARTIN: You love me?
SHARON: Don't rush me –

INT. MAIN HALLWAY. PRE-DAWN
The loathsome kiss seems to last for ever.
MARY: You do love me, Jack.
JACK: Yes . . .
　　(*Her face is regaining its beauty, as the kiss goes on.*)
MARY: Look at me, Jack.
　　(*He opens his eyes. He sees* MARY *as the beautiful waif he first
　　encountered.*)

72

INT. MARY'S ROOM. PRE-DAWN
SHARON *rushes towards the window into* MARTIN'S *arms.*
MARTIN: For ever –
SHARON: Any way you want it.
    (*She reaches for him, coming forwards. But he is insubstantial
    and she crashes through the window, falling into the night
    outside. She cries out.*)
    MARTIN!!!

EXT. CASTLE. DAWN
SHARON *falls through the air, towards the cobblestones below.*

INT. MAIN HALLWAY. DAWN
JACK *goes to kiss* MARY *again, but a terrifying scream is heard
outside, from* SHARON. MARY *vanishes in his arms.*

EXT. LAKE. DAWN
PLUNKETT, *standing by the lakeside, sees the last fireflies die over
the water.*
PLUNKETT: 'Our revels are now ended . . .'
    (*He turns and sees the Americans clinging in terror to the
    trees.*)

INT. MAIN HALLWAY. DAWN
JACK *runs to the doors, panic-stricken.*
JACK: Sharon! Mary!

EXT. CASTLE. DAWN
JACK *emerges. He sees* SHARON's *body huddled on the
cobblestones.*
JACK: Oh, my God. What have I done?
    (*From the trees come* PLUNKETT *and the Americans and
    Irish.*)
MARGE: Where did they all go?
PLUNKETT: Don't ask me. He's the expert.
MALCOLM: It's your bloody castle.
MARGE: Maybe they're not gone yet –
    (*They come upon* JACK, *bending over* SHARON's *body.*)

73

JACK: (*To the body*) You weren't meant for me. But you weren't meant for this either.
(*The body shifts. A hand reaches out and touches his.*)
Sharon. My God . . .
(*The hand touches his face. He looks down and sees* MARY *gazing at him, alive, and now fully human.*)
MARY: For ever, Jack.
(JACK *kisses her. Ecstasy. Then –*
JACK: But where's Sharon?

INT. MARY'S BEDROOM. DAWN
SHARON *and* MARTIN *in bed.*

SHARON: Come off it. How can I be dead?

MARTIN: Take my word for it.

SHARON: You're just saying that so you can have your wicked
    way with me.
    (MARTIN *embraces her.*)

MARTIN: You said for ever.

SHARON: I know, but this is ridiculous. (*She laughs with
    pleasure.*) RIDICULOUS!!!

EXT. CASTLE. DAY
PLUNKETT *and* KATIE *stand arm in arm, watching* EAMON *load
up the Americans' luggage in a hired limo.* TONY *and* MIRANDA
come out of the castle, holding hands.

PLUNKETT: You forgot your collar, Brother Tony.

MIRANDA: No, he didn't. He threw it away. Didn't you, baby?
    (TONY *beams.* MIRANDA *kisses him. They get into the limo.
    The Clays come out of the castle.*)

MALCOLM: Plunkett, this is single-handedly the worst vacation
    I've ever had in my entire life.

PLUNKETT: Thank you, Mr Clay.

MALCOLM: However, if it makes you feel any better, I will be
    recommending Castle Plunkett as the most haunted place
    on earth. I don't imagine that will hurt business any.

PLUNKETT: You're too kind.
    (*The Clays get into the limo.*)

INT. MRS PLUNKETT'S ROOM. DAY
MR *and* MRS PLUNKETT *watch the limo pull away. They raise
their sherry glasses and toast one another.*

INT. MAIN HALLWAY. NIGHT
Late at night, an old radio is playing swing music. JACK *and*
MARY *are dancing cheek to cheek by the fire, a glass of champage in
hand.*

MARY: I cannot thank you enough, Sir Jack, for deciding to stay.

JACK: It was nothing, and when are you going to stop calling
    me sir?

MARY: Sorry –

JACK: When you marry me?

MARY: Are you asking?
>   (*Suddenly a magnificent waltz drowns out the radio. A ghostly*
>   MARTIN *and* SHARON *dance in, resplendently dressed.*)
>   Not again!
JACK: (*To* SHARON) Can't we have a little privacy?
SHARON: The day is for you. The night for me . . .
JACK: Sharon –
>   (*She breaks from* MARTIN *and begins to dance with* JACK.)
SHARON: How's the corpse?
JACK: Great. How's the psycho?
SHARON: He's a pussycat. So, it was worth the trip, eh?
JACK: Yeah. Sharon, I'm sorry things didn't work out, but –
>   (MARY *and* MARTIN *dance.*)
MARTIN: It's such a relief not to have to kill you every
>   night . . .
MARY: It must be a great burden off you . . .
SHARON: Keep smiling, Jack, and don't step on my toes –
>   (*She lets go of him and resumes dancing with* MARTIN.)
>   My only reason for dying, my love . . .
>   (*They dance into the shadows and vanish.* JACK *and* MARY
>   *stare after them.*)
JACK: How'd she learn to dance like that?
MARY: Happiness, Sir Jack.
JACK: Ah.
>   (*He takes her in his arms and dances elegantly.*)
>   Happiness.
>   (*The camera cranes higher and higher on* JACK *and* MARY
>   *below, as* MARTIN *and* SHARON *dance magically through the
>   upper turrets.*)